THE
MIDNIGHT
WIFE

L.G. DAVIS

The Midnight Wife
L.G. Davis
Copyright © 2019
All Rights Reserved.

Cover design: The Cover Collection

For my husband.

CHAPTER 1

I open the oven door and a cloud of heat is released into the air around me.

Jared walks into the kitchen just as I'm removing the chicken and potatoes gratin dish from the oven.

"Perfect." He rubs his hands together. "Just like you. My perfect little wife." He crosses the space between us and gives me a kiss on the side of my neck. Fresh out of the shower, he smells of aftershave and soap.

"No one's perfect," I say, pretending I'm not flattered.

He gives me time to lower the hot dish onto the granite countertop and turns me to face him. "Then I guess I'm the luckiest man in the world."

My chest aches as I place a hand on his cheek, enjoying the feel of his stubble against my palm. His moss green eyes gaze deep into my soul and my heart moves from its usual place.

At first sight, Jared might not seem

particularly handsome, but his good looks emerge the longer one looks at him. His eyes, full lips, and aquiline nose are his best features. At thirty-seven, there's not a wrinkle in sight. I'm five years younger and fine lines have already started to appear around my eyes.

If he only knew how wrong he is about me being perfect. He has no idea how far from perfect I am.

"We've only been married for fifteen months, Mr. Bloom. We're still in the honeymoon phase. Will you still feel the same way about me five or ten years from today?"

He presses a kiss to my lips, leaving behind the cool aftertaste of peppermint sugar-free chewing gum. "Don't complicate things by thinking too far into the future." His warm hand covers mine. "Let's live for the moment."

I don't say anything more, content to stand with my husband in the middle of our kitchen, surrounded by the mouthwatering aromas of chicken, spices, and cheese.

I can't believe how lucky I am to be married to Jared. He's the first person to ever think I'm perfect. I'm determined to spend the rest of my life trying to prove that he's right.

The illusion of perfection is what keeps me safe, an invisible cloak that hides the scars and secrets. Being perfect keeps me organized, and being organized prevents me from making mistakes.

I follow Jared to the dining room. Together we lay out everything on the table, which is far too big for two people.

The only time we use it is when we have guests, which is every two weeks. Jared likes to have his friends over, and they love my cooking.

I'm not an outgoing person by nature. The company of too many people makes me anxious. But I do it because it makes him happy.

It's a small price to pay for what he has done for me, for giving me a life I never thought I could have. I would do anything to keep this life.

It's risky to invite people into our home, but it would be suspicious if I kept them at a distance. The residents of Sanlow, Montana, treat each other like one big family.

I have no choice but to hide in plain sight.

Before the guests arrive, Jared tells me to go and take a shower, and to wear the dress he put out for me on the bed, a bright red cocktail dress with a strip of black lace trimming the collar and hem.

"You look amazing," he says, handing me a pair of shiny, black velvet pumps.

I would have felt more comfortable in a pair of jeans, a plain t-shirt, and no shoes on my feet. But we have an unspoken rule in our marriage. Whenever we go out or meet people, Jared chooses what I wear.

He tells me he has a good sense of style and he likes me to look my best in front of his friends. That's why when we got married, my wedding present was a whole new wardrobe. For a girl who came to town with only a backpack, I was blown away.

At the start of our marriage, it was fun when he chose what I wore. Now I wish I had more control over my clothing.

I keep telling myself it's fine. At least when I'm home alone, I'm free to wear what I like.

The first time I refused to wear what he chose for me, he locked himself inside his home office and threw stuff at the wall.

He has a temper, but he often lets it run its course behind closed doors. When it passes, he walks out, all smiles as if nothing happened, as if he's not the same person who had stormed off.

Sometimes I crave to know him better. After three months of dating and one year of marriage, I still don't know him well.

All I know is that he was an only child and his parents died soon after he graduated from high school. Every time I want to know more, he changes the subject.

I don't hold it against him. I'm a stranger to him too. He just doesn't know it.

I push my feet into new shoes, inwardly wincing because they're too tight around the toes. When I'm done, I pick up a ponytail holder from the dresser.

"Wear your hair down," he says, leaning against the doorframe. "I like it that way."

"Okay." I lower my lashes to hide my disappointment and reach for a boar-bristle brush to run it through my long black hair.

As soon as I'm done, he nods with approval. "Perfect as always," he says with a smile.

Before I can say anything, the doorbell rings.

"I'll get it." He runs downstairs to let the guests in.

We always invite the same people over, three of Jared's friends and their wives.

Before I leave the room, I pull in several breaths, steeling myself for the conversations and the stares, especially from Victor Hanes, Jared's best friend, a surgeon who lives next door. I don't like the way he looks at me. It disgusts me that he always takes every opportunity to flirt with me even though we're both married.

My discomfort is safely tucked away when I enter the dining room. Everyone is already settled in, laughing and talking with drinks in their hands.

"Wow," Linda Jennings says. "You look amazing, Kelsey." As the wife of Don Jennings, a successful lawyer, she always strives to look better than everyone else, but thanks to Jared dressing me up, she has competition. She glances at the other women in the room. "It's hard not to look like a frump next to her, right?"

"You all look great," I say, ignoring the burn at the back of my throat. They're all dressed casually in jeans or shorts, and simple blouses. I'm sure Jared has told them again that it's a casual dinner party. I have a feeling he does that because he likes me to stand out.

The other wives also compliment me, except for Rachel, Victor's wife, who is always reserved and quiet, only speaking when she's spoken to, using only a few words. I always get the feeling that she doesn't like me.

She's beautiful in a fragile way, with pale skin and hair so blonde it's almost white. I've seen her smile only a handful of times since the day I met her, when Jared introduced me to her and Victor. Sometimes I wonder whether she's unhappy, but it's none of my business.

As everyone settles around the tempered glass and chrome dining table, I'm still on my feet, making sure they have everything they need. As soon as I place the food in front of them, I walk out again.

Jared's gaze follows me out of the room. He hates it when I disappear during a meal. He wants me to sit there with everyone staring at me.

Inside the guest bathroom, I close the door and lean against it, drawing in deep breaths until my heart settles.

"Keep it together, Kelsey," I whisper to my reflection in the illuminated LED mirror. "You're lucky to have this life. Don't mess it up."

I force a smile and step out of the room to join the others, to pretend I'm the perfect host.

"This food is absolutely delicious," Linda says, slicing into her goat cheese terrine. "How is it that everything you cook is pure perfection?"

"I do the best I can," I say.

They have no idea that before the dinners I spend hours flipping through cookbooks and scrolling through online recipes. Sometimes I cook the meals first before serving them at a dinner. Jared always appreciates the efforts I put in. He gets to taste all the meals before anyone else.

"Forget the perfect food," Connie chirps. She's the wife of Lewis Shay, a pharmacist who never says much. "How do you create such a perfect life?"

"Come on, Connie," I say. "Perfect is an illusion." I cover my words with forced laughter.

"I'm a lucky man to be able to live in her world." Jared lowers his fork to his plate and reaches for my hand, squeezing it. "I couldn't have chosen a better wife."

"You are indeed one lucky man," Victor says, his beady eyes on my face.

My skin prickles as I pull my gaze from his. Since the day Jared introduced us, I felt uncomfortable in his presence. There's something about him that rubs me the wrong way.

Maybe it's the way he looks at me as though he can see right through me, peeling away the layers. Or maybe it's the way he smiles as though he's trying to tell me something without words. Whatever the case, I don't trust him.

I manage to steer the conversation from myself to the weather and the upcoming Flower Festival that takes place once a year in Sanlow.

As I speak to the others, I focus on one person at a time. It's safer that way. It allows me to keep in control, to measure my words before they leave my lips.

Speaking to lots of people makes me nervous. I live in constant fear of saying the wrong thing at the wrong time, to the wrong person.

I focus on one person, but I'm aware of all the other conversations.

I catch most words and strain my ears to hear the whispers. My eyes scan their faces, searching for words that have not been said. I'm a part of every conversation without actively participating.

"Are the twins having fun at their new kindergarten?" I ask Linda, who is sitting to my left.

She waits until she has chewed the food in her mouth and looks at me with a smile that has been whitened and brightened at the local beauty parlor.

"Now they are." She sighs. "The first few weeks were hell with me having to pick them up after every fifteen minutes. I swear, it took two weeks before they let me stay away for longer. But now they stay for two hours and that's perfect for me."

"That's great," I say, lifting a glass of water to my lips, and taking a sip. "Now you will have more time to yourself."

Linda, like all of us women at the table, is a housewife. We live to create the perfect homes for ourselves and our husbands. But I have only one reason for being a housewife and that's because looking for a long-term job is too risky. What if the employers dig into my past?

Thankfully, Jared prefers it. Even though he doesn't earn too much from his job as a firefighter, he has a lot of money saved, enough to support both of us.

"Absolutely," Linda says. "I thought this day would never come." She laughs out loud, throwing her head back so her auburn curls tumble down her back. "Now I can actually go to the bathroom without being followed by a little person."

I nod with a tiny smile. I'll never be able to experience the joys or pains of motherhood. Before we got married, Jared and I decided that we don't want kids.

Linda changes the subject and starts talking about how she's renovating the master bedroom for the second time in eight months, then she starts complaining that Don travels too often and she feels like a single mom sometimes.

I listen without giving my input. I personally love it when Jared travels because on those days I'm not told what to wear or how to act. Even though I love my husband, when he's away I can actually be myself. There's no pressure for me to be perfect all the time. But Jared hardly travels and when he does, he doesn't stay away for longer than two or three days.

Sometimes I wonder how long I'll be able to keep up this illusion. How long will it be until I crack?

Linda speaks until the main meal is gone and I stand up to get the dessert.

"Do you need help?" Jared asks, pushing back his own chair.

"No, sweetheart. I'll be fine." It's my chance to be alone again for a few minutes, to calm my nerves.

Inside the kitchen, I take a quick calming breath and get started with decorating the two key lime pies with cream and thin slices of lime. The tangy scent curls upward to bring my sense of smell to life.

Before carrying them to the dining room, I clutch the edge of the kitchen counter to take more deep breaths, my eyes squeezed shut as I fill my lungs with air.

"Are you all right?" someone asks from behind me. I spin around.

It's Linda.

"Yes, yes, of course." I straighten up and smile.

"I didn't mean to startle you." She glances at the pies and shakes her head. "Seriously, how do you do it? What's your secret?"

"I don't know what you mean."

"I mean, everything about you is perfect. You cook the best food, you have the best body, and your home is always spotless."

It amuses me that Linda doesn't think she has a gorgeous body, even though after having two kids, she looks amazing.

I shake my head. "That's because I don't have kids. If I did, I'm sure the house would be a mess." Heat floods my cheeks. "I'm not saying that your home—"

"Well, my home *is* a mess. You're right, kids have a way of turning a house upside down. I've actually stopped cleaning while they're awake. It's a waste of time." She pauses. "Should I help you take the dessert into the dining room?"

"Thank you." I lift one of the pies from the counter and hand it to her. "I'll bring the other."

She leaves, and when I think I'm alone, Victor strides through the door.

15

He stands in the doorway, observing me in silence.

"Hi, Victor, do you need anything?" I ask. He's a few steps from me and I'm already finding it hard to breathe.

"I came to offer my help." He steps closer into the room, toying with the full beard on his chin.

"That's kind of you, but I don't need help."

"Everyone needs help." His eyes linger on my face for too long.

When he doesn't look away, I grab a pie and hand it to him.

I find it strange that he came to help. I've heard from Linda that Rachel told her that Victor never does anything around the house, that he doesn't even seem to know where the kitchen is. It's clear to me that he has other reasons for coming to my kitchen.

"Thank you for your help," I say.

Instead of answering in words, he winks and turns to walk out, almost colliding with Jared who just entered the room. The two men exchange a quick glance before Victor walks away.

Jared doesn't say a word to me until Victor is out of earshot.

He comes to me and places a finger underneath my chin, tilting it upward so my eyes meet his. "What were you two talking about?"

His expression is devoid of emotion.

My stomach clenches while my lips curl into a smile that does not reach my eyes. "Nothing. He offered to help."

"But you were laughing." He drops his hand to his side. "What was that about?"

I frown. "I didn't...I don't remember laughing."

"You *did* laugh," he says and just like that, he walks out of the kitchen, leaving me confused.

The rest of the evening flies by. Jokes are shared, laughter is heard, the dessert is enjoyed, and finally they all leave and I breathe a sigh of relief. My relief is momentary. As soon as the front door is closed, Jared storms to his office and slams the door.

Things start to break.

It's a good thing he always cleans up his own mess.

An hour later, he comes to bed and drapes an arm around me. He falls asleep before I do.

At midnight, my anxiety reaches its peak, and as usual, I sneak out of bed and go downstairs to clean the kitchen until my inner demons are silenced.

CHAPTER 2

"I'm going to the gym, honey," I call out to Jared an hour after we've had a quiet dinner at our kitchen table.

He's inside his office catching up on paperwork. He's not angry today. The door is open. He only closes it whenever he's fuming.

"Is it a good idea for you to work out on a full stomach?" He emerges from the office and meets me at the top of the stairs. He has a smile on his face.

"I didn't eat much. I only had a small salad."

I push myself to my tiptoes and kiss him. He tastes of the strawberries he ate for dessert. "I won't be long."

"Take your time. I have work to distract me." He tucks a lock of my hair behind my ear. "Have a good time. I wish you wouldn't wear those leggings though. You know I don't like you looking sexy when I'm not with you." He twirls me around.

"Come on, Jared. I'm wearing leggings and a large t-shirt, and it's a gym for women."

Please don't make me change clothes.

"Fine." He sighs. "It's getting dark. Come straight home when you're done."

"I will." I turn to walk away, his gaze following me down the steps.

Jared always has to know where I am. The days he doesn't reach me are the ones he locks himself in his office.

Downstairs, I'm about to wear my shoes when I glance out the window.

The sun is setting on the other side of the glass. The scene is so breathtaking that I instantly change my mind about going to the gym. I'll go for a run along the lake instead.

I consider going back upstairs to tell Jared I've changed my mind, but I can hear his muffled voice from a distance. He must be on the phone. I wouldn't want to disturb him.

Following my bliss, I abandon the gym bag and run out the door.

As I run along the pavement, the hairs at the back of my neck rise.

I throw a gaze at Victor and Rachel's living room window in time to see the sheer curtains twitch.

Someone is always watching, especially in a small town like Sanlow. Everyone knows everyone's business. It's dangerous for a person with secrets.

I run faster, my feet hitting the ground hard until I reach the small path leading to the lake.

I run at least once a week because it keeps me sane. Getting my blood pumping and my lungs burning reminds me that I'm alive.

When I met Jared and fell deeply in love, I thought my chance at happiness had arrived. He made me feel special for the first time in my life. Marrying him was my chance to start over. I thought we would be happy forever.

We *are* happy, I tell myself every day, but he's slowly starting to suffocate me. But I choose not to worry about that tonight, not when I have such beautiful nature to admire.

Lake Sanlow is one of the largest and most spectacular lakes in the US and it's a stone's throw from our home.

As soon as I reach the man-made beach, I come to a halt and inhale the fresh scent of freedom and wildflowers while listening to the sounds of buzzing insects.

I spend a few minutes gazing out at the sparkling water. Its hold on me is so strong that I get close to the edge where it licks the dry sand.

When the wind picks up and chills my skin, I wrap my arms around my body and continue to watch the sun lower beyond the horizon. With each breath, any tension in my body melts away.

I close my eyes and allow the breeze to caress

my skin, brushing the hair from my face, calming me down, embracing me with all my flaws.

As air rushes into my lungs I stretch out my hands on both sides of me and pretend I'm flying.

After a while, I drop my arms again and start running toward my favorite spot, a place where a small river breaks away from the big lake and branches out on its own, framed by lush vegetation and wildflowers. It's far, but the peace I find there is always worth it.

I make it to my little piece of heaven after a thirty-minute run, breathless but exhilarated. Sinking onto the slightly damp sand, I wrap my arms around my legs, drawing my knees to my chest.

The sound of the water trickling soothes my nerves. I stay until the night starts to thicken.

Ready to leave, I push myself back to my feet and turn to run back home. Jared has always warned me about going for a run when it's dark outside.

I keep reminding him that Sanlow is a safe town with nice people, but he tells me that even the nicest people can turn dangerous in the blink of an eye.

When fire erupts in my lungs, I slow down to a walk, a smile on my face.

My smile wavers when a twig snaps and the sound of footsteps reaches my ears. I glance behind me to see a man emerging from the bushes, at least I think it's a man given that he has a large build.

Nervous, I break into a run. Knowing I'm not alone at the lake feels like an invasion of my privacy, as if the lake belongs to me.

I don't look behind me again until someone speaks.

"Kelsey? Kelsey, wait." I recognize the voice immediately. I don't need to look to know it's Victor.

I keep running, pretending I didn't hear him as panic wells up inside my throat.

Unfortunately, he's fast. Not long after he calls my name, he catches up with me.

"Hey," he says, breathless. "Didn't you hear me? I was calling."

"Oh, sorry. I didn't...I didn't hear you." I don't stop running.

I'm not interested in speaking to him. If I had remembered to bring my phone, I would have stuck earphones into my ears, pretending to listen to music.

Victor continues to run alongside me. If he makes me uncomfortable indoors, he certainly terrifies me outdoors. After the dinner three days ago, I've decided to make an effort in distancing myself from him.

"It's nice to see you out here. We never get a chance to talk. Jared is always lurking around."

My mind instantly takes me back to when I left the house and saw the curtain on Victor and Rachel's living room window twitching. Was it him watching me? Did he follow me?

"Yeah," I say simply. I don't even glance at him. Best to keep going, focus on my destination. Home.

"I didn't know you're a jogger." He coughs. "Now I know the secret to your great little body. You look stunning as always."

"Victor," I say between clenched teeth. "That's not an appropriate thing to say about your best friend's wife."

"Like anyone else, I'm free to exercise my freedom of speech."

Instead of responding, I pick up my pace.

"Since we're both out here at the same time, maybe we can have a chat. I've always been curious about you. You intrigue me."

As his words sink in, cold dread showers my back.

"I prefer to jog alone, Victor. In silence. I hope you don't mind."

"Ouch. I have to say you're hurting my feelings. There's no reason why you can't jog and chat with me at the same time. I hear women are great at multitasking."

"Look, I don't have time. I need to get home to my husband. I'm sure he's worried." I kick myself inwardly for not bringing my phone.

Jared won't be happy.

"Hey, hey, don't be like that." He shoots out a hand and grabs my wrist, bringing me to a halt. I catch a whiff of booze detaching from his body to plug my nostrils. "Why are you always running from me?"

"I don't know what you're talking about." I glance down at his fingers around my wrist and snatch my hand away. "What are you doing?"

"I just want to have a short conversation with you. Like I said, it's not often that we have enough time to talk to each other alone."

"I don't know what we need to talk about. You should get back to your wife and I should go home to Jared."

I run again, blood pounding in my ears.

At first, he doesn't follow and I'm fooled into thinking he has given up, but his footsteps soon slam hard against the ground. It doesn't take long for him to catch up.

"Can I be honest?" he asks. "Jared is my best friend, but sometimes I hate him for having you." He clears his throat. He's always clearing his throat as though something is constantly stuck inside. "I'm sure you know why. You're hot as hell. Any guy would be jealous."

"Leave me alone, Victor." Sweat trickles into my eyes, making them sting. I hate that we're still at an isolated part of the lake, surrounded by nothing but bushes.

"I don't understand why you have to get home so fast."

"I need to prepare dinner."

"Don't lie to me. You already had dinner. I saw you through the window. You cooked spaghetti tonight, didn't you?"

If I wasn't afraid before, I sure am now. I was right to be uncomfortable around him. He's a creep. How long has he been watching me without my knowledge?

"It's late. I have to go." I run faster, as fast as my legs will allow, my muscles screaming for me to slow down, my knees threatening to give way. Over the sound of my thudding heart, small animals scamper through the nearby bushes, sensing the danger.

"I just have one question for you." He draws nearer to me until I'm able to smell his sweat. "Your name is not really Kelsey, is it?"

His words hit me like a bunch of bricks. I screech to a halt. My body folds forward and my hands grip my knees. I need to be careful about how I respond.

"I don't know what you mean." I force the words through my tight throat. I try to move, but my feet refuse to obey. I'm rooted to the spot.

"It makes me feel better to know you're not as perfect as Jared makes you out to be."

"What are you're talking about?" The intense desire to get away from him brings life back to my limbs and I push myself forward.

"You know exactly what I'm talking about. That's why you look so scared." He comes closer. "What are you hiding, Kelsey? Everyone thinks you're perfect, but you aren't, are you?" He plants himself in front of me so I have no choice but to stop.

"What do you want from me?" I clench my hands at my sides.

"An incentive, that's all. If you don't want me to tell everyone. I could always bring it up at one of your little dinner parties." He shakes his head. "Look, I just want to help you save your squeaky-clean reputation."

He reaches out to touch my cheek. I slap his hand away. As though that's all the permission he needs to put his hands on me, he grabs me by the shoulders and shoves me hard in the direction of the bushes.

"Don't be stupid, Kelsey, or whatever your name is. As it stands, I hold your life in my hands. Give me what I want and I'll allow you to continue living your perfect little lie. My price is low compared to what you'll pay if I expose you."

"Get out of my way." The words come out of my mouth broken. I hate myself for showing him my weakness. He can sense my fear and it's giving him power over me.

"You look so beautiful when you're scared."

He chuckles and shoves me again, so hard that this time I lose my balance and land in the bushes.

I try to scramble to my feet again, but he falls over me, grabbing a handful of my hair.

Before I can recover from the pain of my hair being pulled from my scalp, the right side of my face comes into contact with the ground...hard.

Darkness takes over.

CHAPTER 3

When I regain consciousness, I find myself inside a nightmare.

I must have been out for a while because a lot has happened.

My leggings are off and Victor is on top of me, his weight pressing my body into the hard, rocky ground.

Shock shoots through me like an electric current.

He's raping me, taking what he wants without my permission.

My shock is soon followed by panic and fear. I close my eyes again so he doesn't see I'm awake.

Drunk with adrenaline and driven by the desire to fight, I don't think twice before reaching out into the dirt to grab anything that can free me from the monster who calls himself my husband's friend.

My fingertips come into contact with a rock

big enough to fill my trembling hand and my fingers curl around it.

Before I can think twice, before fear can take over, I slam it hard into his temple.

First, he stiffens with surprise, then he falls forward. Air bursts from my lungs when his chest collides with mine.

"Get off me," I murmur, my throat thick with tears. Before he can recover, I push him off and scramble to my feet.

My body instantly remembers the pain of my head striking the ground.

I sway a little, but I soon catch my balance and pick up my leggings from the ground.

I need to get away from him. I have to get home before he recovers.

Ignoring the sharp pain slicing its way through my brain, I get dressed. I don't know why, but instead of dropping the rock on the ground, I throw it into the lake and run as fast as I can on shaky knees. I don't look back to see if he's coming after me until I reach the sandy beach.

My eyes search the darkness, but I don't see him. I don't hear him. I must have hit him hard enough to keep him on the ground for a while until I make it home.

As I stumble into the small path leading to Montlake Street, the physical pains in my body merge with the emotional kind, gathering into one big ball of fire in the pit of my belly, bringing on painful cramps that almost paralyze me.

The side of my face is starting to throb with pain that shoots into my right eye and almost blinds me, but the pain cannot be compared to that between my legs, the reminder of what happened to me.

I clutch my side until I reach Montlake Street. As hot, angry air bursts from my lungs, I'm grateful that the strcct is isolated. People are inside their homes with their families, safe and sound, unaware of the evils outside. I don't want anyone to see me like this, broken and dirty. I hope nobody is watching without my knowledge.

As soon as I reach our house, I quietly let myself in, but I remain in the entrance hall for a minute or two listening for Jared. It's hard to hear anything with blood pounding in my ears and my body buzzing with agony.

But my ears soon make out his distant voice. He must still be inside his office. My shoulders sink with relief.

I have a few minutes to clean myself up before he sees me. I can't let him see me this way. I don't even know how to tell him what happened.

Holding my breath, I hurry upstairs to the bathroom next to our bedroom and lock myself inside.

I stand in the middle of the bathroom, surrounded by all the beautiful things Jared has given me. The marble, the chandelier, the vintage vanity table, little and big luxuries. I no longer see their beauty. Everything is broken. Nothing will ever be the same again.

I'm not sure how long I stand frozen in one place, but eventually life returns to my limbs and I come back to my senses.

Sucking in a deep breath that scratches my lungs and throat, I shuffle to the shower. I get in fully clothed and allow the hot water to cascade over me. It's only after I'm completely drenched that I peel off my clothes and allow them to pool at my feet. I stand naked under the hot water, my tears mixing with it.

When memories of Victor torture me, I turn up the temperature, wishing I could scald away the dirt and the shame. I wish I could peel off the skin that Victor touched.

I should go straight to the cops to report the rape. That's what a normal person would do. But when you have secrets, cops are your worst enemies.

Victor was right. I'm not who everyone thinks I am. Now I don't know how long it will be until my cover is blown, until someone else knows.

More tears come. I slide to the floor, giving myself the permission to break apart.

My hand moves to my swollen right cheek. My fingertips touch the tender skin. It hurts. Everything hurts like hell. But I need to pull myself together before Jared figures out I'm inside the house and comes looking for me.

Groaning with pain, I push myself to my feet again and scrub my body as best I can.

After scrubbing like a maniac until my skin is raw and red, I step out of the shower. Thick steam releases into the entire bathroom. It clouds every surface.

Forcing myself to remain calm, I put on a fluffy morning robe and approach the medicine cabinet, where I pull out the bottle of disinfectant and a Band-Aid kit.

I take my time treating the wound on my cheek, disinfecting it before covering it up, hiding it from the world. Despite the pain, the cut is not as bad as it feels. The worst pain cannot be seen.

When I'm done, I push back my shoulders and leave the bathroom, pretending I'm not a wreck inside.

I find Jared downstairs in the kitchen, getting himself a glass of water. When he sees me, he frowns.

"What happened?" he asks, his brows drawing together. "Are you hurt?"

I shake my head. "It's nothing. I had a small accident at the gym." The lie tastes bitter on my tongue.

"Should I take a look at it?" He takes a few steps toward me and puts his hands on my shoulders. "I didn't even know you were home."

"I arrived a few minutes ago. You were on the phone. I didn't want to disturb you." A nervous laugh escapes my lips. "Don't worry about me. It's a small cut. Nothing serious. As you can see, I took care of it."

For a split second, I consider telling Jared everything, but I can't get myself to. I don't want him to look at me differently.

The first time he saw me, he made me feel normal, perfect, undamaged. But if he knew the truth about me, he might walk away.

"It's Friday night and I'm not working tonight," he says when he's sure I'm all right. "Should we watch a movie?"

"That would be nice. I'll bring out the snacks."

I don't want to watch a movie. I want to curl up in our bed and weep.

"Sounds great. I'll find a movie for us." He leaves the kitchen with his glass of water and I open the snack cabinet.

I feel nothing as I pour chips and nuts into bowls, my body numb as though it has been switched off.

I finally make it to the living room and sit down next to my husband. Like a normal couple, we eat our snacks and watch a black and white movie. But only my body is in the room. My mind is far away, still at the lake with Victor.

The image of him on top of me makes my

stomach turn. I taste bile at the back of my throat, but I swallow it down before it escapes my mouth.

The movie ends without me knowing what it was about. Luckily, Jared is too exhausted to discuss it. We both stand up and go to the bedroom, where I lie in my husband's arms, wishing he could protect me. Without knowing what happened, he won't be able to.

At midnight, I wake up as usual. This time, the nightmare that wakes me is from the present, not the past.

To get back my control, I do what I do best. I get out of bed and clean. I start with the guest bathroom downstairs, then I move to the living room, where I clean up the mess we made while watching the movie.

When I'm done, my chest is lighter and I'm breathing easier. Unable to return to bed, I sink onto the couch and sit with my head in my hands.

"Kelsey?" Jared says from the doorway and my head snaps up.

"Hey," I say, breathless. "Why are you awake? It's late."

"I got a call." He comes to sit next to me. "It was Rachel. Apparently, Victor didn't come home after he went jogging after dinner." Jared's face is pale and I can see that he's clearly worried.

His words strike me like a bolt of lightning.

Why didn't Victor return home? What if he didn't wake up after I hit him? Did I even hit him that hard? The only thing on my mind was getting as far away from him as possible. I wasn't interested in the extent of his injuries.

"Oh, my God," I say. "How's Rachel?"

"Worried. But then again Victor says she worries about everything. I told her he could be at the hospital, maybe called in for an emergency surgery. She refused to believe it." Jared sighs. "I'll go and check up on her."

"Do you want me to come?"

"No. Don and Linda are going there as well. Let's not overwhelm her with too many visitors. We'll wait with her. I'm sure Victor will show up. You go to bed."

Sleep is the last thing on my mind.

"Okay," I say. I'm so relieved that he doesn't want me to accompany him. The thought of being inside my rapist's house makes me feel sick.

Jared leaves and doesn't return for over an hour. When he finally does, he looks even more pale and his hair and t-shirt are rumpled.

"What happened? Did he come home?"

He shakes his head. "And we called the hospital. He wasn't called in. I came to let you know that we're all going to search the beach. The cops won't do anything until twenty-four hours have passed." He pulls me close. "I'm glad you didn't go jogging tonight."

My stomach twists when I remember that I didn't tell him I changed my mind about going to the gym. Now doesn't feel like the right time to bring it up.

"Me too," I murmur. He has no idea how much I regret going for a run. What seemed like a small insignificant decision has changed everything.

"I need to get a flashlight from the basement."

"Get me one as well. I'm coming with." I lift myself from the couch.

Two hours later, it's 3:00 a.m., and many people from our neighborhood have searched the beach. Victor was nowhere to be found.

When Jared and I enter the house, we are both exhausted and I'm confused. How is it possible that Victor just disappeared into thin air? I had shined my light on the spot I'd left him and found nothing. It actually looked undisturbed.

Where is he and what does it mean for me?

"I don't understand why he would do something so stupid, to disappear without an explanation. Especially since he knows that Rachel likes to worry."

"Maybe he told her he's going somewhere and she forgot." I don't know what else to say to make sense of the situation.

"But he's not answering my calls." Jared strokes his chin. "I hope he's not out doing something stupid."

"Like what?" I asked casually.

"Never mind." Jared turns to me and pulls me close. "Hopefully, he'll turn up."

"Yeah," I say, biting my lower lip. "Let's hope so." I want him to turn up for Rachel's sake, but not for mine. I never want to see the man again.

Back in our bed, I don't sleep at all. I stay awake for most hours of the night, thinking about every possible scenario that has to do with Victor's disappearance. Many questions swirl through my mind, but I don't find any answers.

I fall asleep an hour or so before the sun comes out.

Jared is the first one to get out of bed. I find him in the kitchen, already ready for his morning shift at the station.

"Did you hear any news about Victor?" I rub the sleep from my eyes.

"I'm afraid not," he says, his face clouded with worry. Would he still be that worried if he knew what Victor did to his wife?

He downs his bitter coffee and rises from the kitchen table. "I'll see you later. Don't leave the house without telling me where you're going."

I nod and kiss his cheek. As soon as he steps through the door, I sink to the floor and finally break apart without anyone watching.

CHAPTER 4

It's been over forty-eight hours and Victor has not turned up. The cops have been unable to locate him.

Several other women from the neighborhood and I are at Rachel's house, trying our best to comfort her.

"I don't understand," she says, shredding a piece of tissue in her lap. "What if he's hurt?"

"Don't think like that, sweetie." Linda reaches for Rachel's hand. "I'm sure he'll turn up at some point."

"It's been two days. He never disappears without telling me where he's going." She purses her lips as tears roll down her cheeks. "It's unlike him."

Being around them makes me uncomfortable. I was probably the last person to see Victor before he disappeared and I can't say a word. I'm sure if I tell the cops what happened, they might be able to track him down. But then I'd have to tell them everything that happened. Everything.

I can't.

There's no way I can go to the cops and tell them everything without getting myself exposed. It's too late now anyway. I've waited too long.

I have to continue pretending I know nothing, that I didn't see Victor that night, that he didn't rape me. It's hard because I can still feel the burn of his touch on my skin.

I feel sorry for Rachel, but deep down, I can't help feeling that Victor would have hurt her even more if he stayed. After what he did to me, I'm sure that he doesn't love her enough.

I pull Rachel into my arms and she leans into me. "It was our fifth wedding anniversary yesterday," she says, her warm tears sinking into my silk blouse.

"I'm so sorry, Rachel." I wish I could tell her the truth, but it would only make her pain worse. Hearing that her husband is a rapist would destroy her. By remaining silent I'm actually doing her a favor.

Rachel pulls away and looks into my eyes. Her brown gaze is so intense that I wonder whether she can see through me. Thankfully, she looks away again and accepts a hug from Theresa, another one of her friends. Her real friends.

"We have to remain hopeful," Theresa says, rubbing her back. "We have to believe that he'll come back with a good explanation."

"Thank you." Rachel breaks the

embrace. "Thank you all for being here."

While the others continue to fuss over her, my mind is running wild. Even though I never want to see Victor again, I need to find out what happened to him. Having him gone puts me at a great disadvantage.

Being in the dark makes me nervous. I keep waiting for the other shoe to drop. I'll never be able to relax if I don't know where he is. He is out there and he knows my secrets.

What if he disappeared because he's worried I might go to the cops to report him? But it doesn't make sense. If he knows my secrets, he'd know I have as much to lose as he does. He knows I'd want to keep my past a secret from everyone, especially Jared.

We spend another hour with Rachel until she politely asks us to leave, saying she wants to take a nap. I'm relieved to finally be able to leave their house. I hate seeing photos of Victor around the house.

My relief is short-lived. When I step out of Victor and Rachel's house, I spot a police car in front of ours.

As I put one foot in front of the other, I'm glad the other wives had left a few minutes before me or they would be asking questions.

Jared's SUV is parked in the driveway next to the cop's car. When I left to go to Rachel, he had still been at work.

Why is he back early?

Stay calm, I say to myself as I open our gate and enter the house, which smells of strong coffee.

I find Jared and the cop in the kitchen with coffee mugs in their hands.

"Sweetheart," Jared calls when he sees me in the doorway. "Come in here for a second."

I move as though I'm wading through water. The kitchen door is only a few steps from the table, but it feels as though I'm traveling the entire world to get to it.

The cop is a man with thick, completely gray hair and a forehead so shiny it looks polished. "I'm Officer Smith," he says, standing up to shake my hand. He's wrapped in the scent of sweat and Old Spice.

I discreetly wipe the palm of my hand on my jeans before offering it to him with a smile. "It's good to meet you, officer."

Jared comes to put an arm around my shoulders. "Sweetheart, Officer Smith is here to find out if we know anything about Victor's whereabouts."

"Oh, okay," I say casually and sink into a nearby chair, not because I want to sit down, but because I'm not sure how long my legs would be able to hold me up. "I'm happy to help with anything." I sound different to my own ears, but I cover my discomfort with a smile.

"Perfect," Officer Smith says. "When was the last time you saw Mr. Hanes?"

"I think it was on the day he disappeared." When I notice I'm fiddling with my pearl earring, I drop my hand. I wouldn't want him to think I'm nervous. "But it was from a distance. He was getting into his car."

Officer Smith taps his fingers against his lips. "And what time of day was that?"

"Around noon, I think."

"And you didn't see him anymore after that?"

I shake my head. "No. I didn't see him or his wife." Before I became Kelsey Bloom, I was a terrible liar. It did not come easy to me at all, but now I'm a professional. If I can lie to a cop, I can lie to anyone.

The officer asks me a few more questions and I answer them as best I can without giving myself away. He doesn't seem suspicious at all and I'm grateful for that.

"Well," he says finally, pushing to his feet. "Thank you for taking the time to speak to me. I have to move on to the next house. Hopefully, we can get some answers by evening."

"Please do your best to find him, officer," Jared says. "Victor would never disappear like that, not without telling his wife he's going."

"We promise to do just that." Officer Smith pushes his notepad into his breast pocket along with the pen. "If you come up with any information that could help with the investigation, please don't hesitate to call."

He hands me his business card because I'm closest to him. I don't even look down at it. Instead, I give him my full attention. Diverting my gaze from him might make him suspicious. "We'll do that," I say.

Jared and I escort him out of the house and watch him get into his car.

"Where were you?" Jared asks, a thin thread of warning in his tone. Does he suspect I might lie to him? "I came home and you were not here. You know I hate it when you lie to me." He slams the door shut.

"I didn't lie." I wrap my arms around me, my insides shaking. He never lays a hand on me, but sometimes his words have the power to unravel me.

"You did," he barks. "You told me you'd be home all day." He narrows his eyes. "Look at you, you're a mess. Why didn't you comb your hair?"

My hand goes to my ponytail. "I left the house in a hurry." I inhale sharply. "The other ladies were visiting Rachel, so I decided to join them." I didn't want to be alone with Rachel.

Jared pins me with his gaze until I squirm with discomfort, then out of nowhere, his lips stretch into a grin. "It's kind of you to visit her." He tucks a strand of hair behind my ear. "Just let me know next time."

"I called you, but you didn't answer your phone."

"Then send me a text next time," he barks. "I need to know where you are. I need to know you're safe."

I nod and keep my mouth shut. In the past I would have tried to assure him that Sanlow is safe, but now I've discovered the dark side to the cozy little town.

As soon as he lets me off the hook, I go to the bathroom to catch my breath. But I forget to close the door. After leaning over the basin for a while, I turn around to find Jared standing there, watching me suspiciously.

"Are you okay?" He narrows his eyes. "You look pale."

"I'm...I'm fine. I just have a migraine. I'll take a painkiller."

"Fine." He turns and walks away.

Alone again, I wonder whether he knows something. The way he looked at me was different. Or it could be that I'm being paranoid.

CHAPTER 5

As I walk down the fresh produce aisle of Green Grocer's, dressed in a turquoise summer dress Jared picked out for me this morning, the hairs at the nape of my neck rise.

It's been two weeks since Victor disappeared and I constantly feel as though I'm being watched.

Holding my breath, I scan the space around me, but everything seems normal. Aside from the locals doing their Friday evening shopping, nothing seems out of the ordinary. No one seems suspicious.

Feeling stupid, I grip the handle of my cart tighter and continue walking. The cart wheels squeak with each movement.

A few heartbeats later, I throw a look over my shoulder again in time to see a man standing about nine or ten steps away from me.

Panic grips my throat.

It's him. Every fiber of my being recognizes

his toxic presence.

The man has the same hair that tapers onto the collar and the same height and broad build as Victor. He even stands the same way, in a slouching kind of way.

Fear scorches my spine as I distance myself from him, my legs threatening to give way.

But where am I running to? Where can I hide?

The only way out of my misery would be to leave Sanlow. But I can't do that. I've created this life. I put too much into it to turn my back on it. I can't leave Jared. Despite his imperfections, he's the only man I have ever truly loved.

With sweat trickling down my spine, I grab everything I need and rush to the checkout area.

Just as I'm handing over the money, I see the man from the fresh produce aisle again. I almost choke with relief.

I was wrong. It's not Victor.

I'm being paranoid again.

The man smiles at me. Not only is he clean-shaven, which Victor is not, his features are softer and kinder. He's far from being a monster.

I return his smile and finish paying for my stuff. I grab the bag and stumble out of the store, my breath coming in quick, ragged gasps.

Inside my Ford Focus, I rest my forehead on the steering wheel and draw in a few deep breaths. Even though it wasn't Victor, he's close. I don't need to see him to know that.

Maybe this was his plan all along. He's punishing me from a distance for rejecting him. He wants to drive me to the brink of madness so I can expose myself without him lifting a finger.

I'm not only afraid that he'll reveal my secrets, I'm terrified of him period. I found out the hard way just what he's capable of. He has left scars on my body that I will carry with me for the rest of my life. Even if they're not visible to the world, they're visible to me. I have nightmares of the rape almost every night.

I lift my head off the steering wheel and push my shoulders back.

Pull yourself together, Kelsey.

I need to be extra careful.

Jared has already been watching me suspiciously. I caught him on several occasions observing me in silence through a hooded gaze. He never says a word, but I still worry that he knows something.

I clasp my hands in my lap, gazing out through the windshield. Holding my breath, I pick up the phone to call Rachel.

She picks up on the fifth ring.

"Hey, Rachel, how are you doing?" Even though we're neighbors, I haven't visited her since the time I was at her place with the ladies. I can't face her alone. But I call her from time to time, not only to find out how she's doing, but to see if she can shed more light on Victor's whereabouts. The pain of guilt burns the back of my throat, but using her is the only way for me to keep myself safe.

"Not good," she says, her words drowning in tears.

"What...what happened?" The words rush out of my mouth.

"He left me," she says softly. "Victor left me."

"I know. I'm so sorry." I don't know what comes over me, but I'm suddenly tearful. Her husband is a monster, but her pain still touches me. Not knowing where he is must be devastating.

"No," she says, her sharp tone slicing the air like a knife. "He actually *did* leave me...our marriage."

"Oh," I say. I don't know what else to say. I need her to continue, but I don't want to seem too eager.

"This morning I got a letter from him."

"He wrote to you? What did the letter say?"

"That he had to go away for a while because he needs time alone to think about his life." She sniffs. "What he means is that he wants to think about our marriage."

It doesn't make sense. He can't be gone if I keep getting the feeling that he's stalking me. He has to be lying to her.

"Oh, Rachel, it doesn't have to mean he walked out on your marriage. Maybe...well, maybe he's going through something and needed to get away to process it. I'm sure he loves you and—"

"That's what he wants you all to think." The force of her seething reply takes me by surprise. I've always known her to be soft-spoken. "Our marriage is not as perfect as everyone thinks. He blames me, you know. He says it's my fault that we're not able to conceive. Before he left, he hardly looked at me anymore, not the way he looks at other women."

"Are you sure the letter is from him?" For obvious reasons, I need to change the subject from the topic of Victor's wandering eyes.

"Don't you think I would recognize my own husband's handwriting?" She inhales sharply. "The letter is definitely from him."

"I'm sorry. I don't mean to upset you." I close my eyes. "I just...do you need anything? Can I do something for you? I'm at Green Grocer's right now. Is there something you need from the store?"

"That's nice of you, Kelsey. But I have everything I need. I'm going out of town for a few days anyway. I'm visiting my mom in Billings."

"That's a good idea. Some time away might do you good." It would be good for me too because I won't feel terrible each time I see her. "If you need anything at all, give me a call. I mean it."

"Don't worry about it. You've done enough." She pauses. "Look, I better get packing. I need to get out of this house. I can't stand to be around his things."

"Okay. Have a safe trip." We end the call and I sit in the car for a long time with the doors locked, unsure what to feel.

I'm still in a daze as I drive home, oblivious to my surroundings. After driving on autopilot, it's a wonder I manage to arrive in one piece.

I dump the grocery bags onto the kitchen counter and stare through the window at the distant lake. My stomach rolls every time I look out. I used to find so much comfort in the view, but now it only reminds me of the horrors of that night.

When I return to the car for another bag of groceries, I find a yellow sticky note on the windshield.

Before I even read the words, my gut tells me it's from him. He's making it clear that he's not going away.

I peel the note from the glass. The words swim in front of my eyes before I can focus my gaze.

I know your little secret. If you don't tell, I will.

I wrap my fingers around the note, crushing it until it's so small I can barely feel it in my hand.

I run back to the house, leaving the rest of the groceries in the trunk. I'm not safe outside. I'm not even sure I'm safe inside my own home.

On my way to our front door, I look everywhere around me, but I don't see him. It doesn't mean he's not watching. After all, he admitted to watching me even when I didn't know it.

As soon as I close the door behind me, bile rushes up my throat. I make it to the bathroom in time for it to flood my mouth and spew out of me into the toilet bowl, some of it coming out of my nose.

When I have retched until there's nothing left inside me, I continue to kneel in front of the toilet, my burning eyes closed, my hand still tight around the crumpled note.

The message is clear.

Victor is out to destroy me. What will be left of me once he's done?

My heart, my body, and every other part of me knows that this is just the beginning. He will hurt me again and there's not a damn thing I can do about it.

I can only suffer in silence until the darkness completely suffocates me.

Nothing is more painful than watching my life falling apart, becoming ashes of what could have been.

CHAPTER 6

Jared leans back in his chair and lifts his cup of coffee to his lips. He drains it in only a few gulps. He never eats breakfast, claiming it makes him feel tired. I've stopped trying to talk him into it.

"Are you okay?" I ask when his eyes search my face as though he's trying to read me. "Why are you looking at me that way?"

He puts down his cup and shakes his head. "Sorry. I was just wondering what would make a man leave his wife out of the blue. I could never do that to you."

"Not even if I did something really terrible?"

"There are different levels of terrible." He pushes his cup aside and lays his hands on the table, palms down. "What I'm saying is, I can't just leave without telling you I'm going. What Victor did to Rachel is messed up."

I lower my gaze to the table to hide the secrets in my eyes. "Have you tried calling him again?"

"A couple of times. His phone keeps going to

voicemail. I guess he's determined to stay away." He drags a palm down the side of his face. "I bet he's in a seedy motel somewhere with some filthy prostitute."

I reach for my avocado and kale smoothie. "Why are you talking as if he's done something like this before?"

"He's run off before. But not without a word, and he has never stayed away this long. When he and Rachel go through a rough patch, he has a habit of searching for comfort in other women's arms." Jared sighs. "He's one of those guys who are incapable of keeping it in their pants."

"Oh." I avert my gaze. "Rachel *did* mention that their marriage wasn't as happy as we thought it was."

The memory of Rachel's phone call a week ago comes hand in hand with an image of the note I found on my car. Even if Victor hasn't sent another one, the words written on the note eat away at me every night.

"No, it wasn't. Victor never made a secret of it, but Rachel kept believing she could change him. But the truth is, she never could. After his bachelor party, I knew exactly what kind of marriage they would have. I'm actually surprised that Rachel is not the one who left him."

I drink a few sips of the creamy smoothie and put down the cool glass. "You're very different, you and Victor. It's amazing that you still manage

53

to be good friends."

Jared shrugs. "When someone gives you a kidney, you owe them your life."

"Yeah, I forgot about that." Jared used to suffer from kidney disease and he did tell me about Victor giving him a kidney to save his life. Apparently, they were not even close friends at the time. It was only a couple of months after Jared moved to Sanlow, six years ago.

At first, I used to be grateful to Victor for what he did for Jared. I thought he was a good person. Until he started flirting with me.

Jared pushes back his chair and gets to his feet. He takes his cup to the sink.

After he rinses the cup and dries his hands, he pulls me to my feet and wraps his arms around my waist, tighter than is comfortable. "Don't you ever leave me, you hear?" he says, his gaze arresting mine. "Don't you dare even think about it."

"The same goes for you." My words come out in a shaky whisper.

"As long as you continue to be my perfect wife, I won't."

His answer makes me as uncomfortable as his arms around my body.

"Don't look so frightened. The ball is in your court, baby. Play by the rules and all will be well." He kisses a corner of my lips, but his warm lips don't melt the ice spreading through my stomach.

I love him and he loves me, but like Rachel and Victor's, our marriage is far from perfect.

When Jared and I met, I was working as a waitress at the Little Meadow, a diner in the center of town. I'd only been working there for a week when he walked in one rainy evening.

Love was not in my plans, but Jared Bloom has a way of getting what he wants, and he wanted me. He came to the diner every night for two weeks until I agreed to go on a date with him. I fell in love after our first date and decided to try my luck with him.

Now here we are and I'm no longer sure if I made the right decision. I never once thought there would come a time when his love would suffocate me.

"I'll see you in the evening," he says with a grin. "I should be done by six. We're going to the movies. It's been a while since we did that. I'll call you later so we can decide on the time."

He walks out of the door before I can come up with a reason why we shouldn't go. It's not that I don't want to go. I do, but a movie theater could be the perfect place for Victor to hide.

After the front door closes, I lock all the doors and windows and prepare to get through the day without coming undone.

As soon as Jared's Ford Explorer pulls out of the garage, I jump into the shower, turning the water to the lowest temperature. I stand under the water, shivering with tears in my eyes, too drained by fear to even wash my body. After the initial bite of cold, my skin adjusts to the temperature and I step out. The cold was only to distract me from the thoughts torturing my mind.

On the way to our bedroom, I hear a sound downstairs. My heart is lodged in my throat as I run into the bedroom and lock the door. Then my gaze lands on the bed and blood drains from my face.

There's a piece of paper on the bed. I'm positive it wasn't there before I went to the bathroom.

It's a headline torn from a newspaper article. I read the fading words, my chest tightening by the second.

The letters jump off the page and slam into my core.

Lacie Pullman the Granny Killer…

My fingers curl around my neck as I struggle to breathe.

Victor wasn't lying. He knows the truth about me. The piece of paper is a sign that he's near, maybe even hiding inside my own house while Rachel is out of town.

He waited for Jared to leave so he could send

me another sign. What if he's still inside the house? What if he wants to rape me again, to break me into even smaller pieces?

I can't let him touch me again.

A wave of dizziness weakens my legs as I hurry to get dressed.

As soon as I'm fully clothed, I check the bedroom door and window to make sure they're still closed. I'll stay in the bedroom until Jared comes home if I have to. I only wish we had an en-suite bathroom. Sooner or later I'll have to use the toilet. Fear has already started to loosen my bladder.

I'm sitting on the bed with an umbrella and an iron next to me, my arms around my legs. My body is rocking back and forth as I search my brain for ways to protect myself.

I dread going to the movies with Jared tonight. I have no doubt now that Victor will be there watching us. I have to call it off.

I reach for my phone and call Jared.

"Sweetie, I don't think I'll be able to make the movies tonight. I just remembered that Linda is coming over this evening. Why don't you go out with your friends tonight?"

"Linda is coming over? That's weird, I spoke to Don and he says she's in Mississippi at a church retreat."

Heat floods my cheeks. Nothing is more embarrassing than being caught in a lie. I should have said I'm sick or come up with another excuse that didn't include anyone. But my mouth spoke before my mind could filter the words.

"Oh. I guess she forgot to cancel. Or maybe she did and I forgot." I press my lips together, my eyes on the door as if I'm waiting for it to be kicked in. "I guess we can go to the movies."

"What's going on, Kelsey? You don't sound like yourself. Is everything all right?"

"I'm tired, that's all. I haven't been sleeping too well lately."

"I know. I always hear you walking around at night."

"You do?" A heavy feeling settles in the pit of my stomach. How much does he see at night? Does he follow me around the house as I move from room to room to clean up the mess that has become my life?

"Yeah, I hear you getting out of bed. But I'm often too tired to keep you company. You clean at night, don't you? The house is always sparkling when I get up in the morning. I should start calling you my midnight wife."

I let out a nervous laugh. "I guess you married a strange woman, huh? When I can't sleep, I think it's a waste of time to sit and wait for morning. I prefer to do something productive." He doesn't have to know about the nightmares that torture me in my sleep.

"I see." His tone is suddenly hard. "I don't

care if you wake up and clean at midnight, but Kelsey, never lie to me again. I'm not a fool. You didn't have plans with Linda and you know it."

CHAPTER 7

Just as I had expected, the small theater is packed with locals and a few tourists.

As we enter, with Jared's arm around my waist, my entire body is on full alert.

It's hard not to look over my shoulders every few seconds. My eyes flicker on every face we come across, searching for my enemy.

I don't find him, but I feel his presence. I still feel his breath on my cheek, his hands on my body. I don't see him, but he continues to invade my private space, disturbing the air I breathe.

"You okay?" Jared asks after we buy our tickets. "Are you still tired?"

After the way we ended the call this morning, with him telling me to never lie to him, I have been nervous about seeing him tonight.

To my relief, he showed up with a smile on his face and swept me into his arms as though nothing happened. How many things did he throw at the wall to rid himself of his anger?

"No, I'm fine. I look forward to seeing *Uptown Pete*." As usual, Jared chose the movie. He gave me three options. I made a choice, but he changed it and made it look as though we arrived at the decision together. I don't get why he asked me in the first place. I actually don't mind watching the movie he chose. It's a romantic comedy and some laughter would do me good right now.

"How about I get us some popcorn? That will cheer you up."

It worries me that he thinks I need cheering up. I need to do a better job at hiding my emotions when he's around. "No popcorn for me today," I say as my eyes peer past his shoulders at a group of men behind him. None of them is Victor.

"No popcorn?" Jared raises an eyebrow. "Since when do you say no to popcorn? Are you sure you're all right?" He lays a hand on my forehead.

I force a smile. "I'm on a diet and popcorn is not allowed. Haven't you noticed all the smoothies I've been drinking?"

Even though Jared thinks I love popcorn, I'm not a fan. It's one of those things he manipulated me into believing I like. Whenever we came to the movies and I refused popcorn, he went on about how it's my favorite thing. In the beginning, I told him I didn't like it, but he refused to accept it until I let it go.

"I don't understand why you need to go on a diet." He scans my body before his gaze returns to my face. "You're perfect. Everyone says so."

"Diets are not only for weight loss, you know. It's for overall health."

"Come on, Kelsey." He chuckles. "A bit of popcorn won't make a difference."

I shrug. "I guess you're right. But I'm feeling lightheaded now. Do you mind if I go in already to find our seats while you get the popcorn and drinks?"

Jared agrees, but as soon as he walks away from me, it hits me that I might have made a mistake. What if I go inside the theater and I'm all alone in there, surrounded by darkness? What if Victor follows me inside?

But if I don't go in, Jared might find it odd since I told him I'm not feeling well.

I take my time walking to theater number 3. I'm relieved to find several people already inside.

Forcing myself to remain calm, I find our seats and lower myself into mine. I glance behind me. Nothing suspicious. Maybe I'm wrong and Victor is not here. Maybe he doesn't even know where we are.

The commercials start and Jared has still not returned. But it's fine because I have started to relax a little.

It would make sense for Victor not to come to the theater. There are too many people who might spot him, especially after he's been away for three weeks. I don't think he wants to be seen. He prefers to remain in the shadows.

When Jared finally appears at my side, I sigh with relief and take his hand. "You're right. I do want popcorn."

For some weird reason, my mouth actually waters when I inhale the warm, buttery aroma. Before now, it used to make me nauseous.

Jared kisses my cheek and pushes his hand into the bag of popcorn, coming out with a handful. I nudge him playfully in the ribs.

"That's too much," I say, a smile sneaking up on me. "This is my popcorn."

"Come on," he says, munching the popcorn. "I'm the one who went to get it. You have to share."

"You should have gotten yourself some."

"I thought when we married, we promised to share everything with each other." He leans in so I can hear his words over the loud sounds coming from the screen.

I only laugh and he joins in. For the first time in a while, I don't feel too tense around him. It reminds me of when we were dating, when things were easy, when he didn't scare me a little. Maybe coming to the movies wasn't such a bad idea. I need a break from my nightmares.

As I lean back in my chair, chewing on my popcorn, which actually tastes delicious, I make myself a silent promise. I promise to be present, to enjoy the time with my husband.

Jared says something to me, but his words are drowned out by the sounds coming from the speakers.

"What did you say?" I lean closer to him.

"I said I'm glad we came tonight," he says louder. "Sorry that I've been so busy lately."

"It's all right." I'm glad he's busy. That way he won't be around to see me come undone.

The movie starts. Ten minutes in, I involuntarily glance behind me again at the dark faces behind us. When I don't see anything to worry me, I turn back to the screen and settle into my seat, pretending everything is normal, that my life is not in shreds.

I don't know what happens, but halfway through the movie, my anxiety sneaks up on me. Nothing out of the ordinary has happened, but suddenly, fear is rearing its ugly head again.

My body tenses and the dormant knot inside my stomach starts to pulse. Even though I want to continue playing the game of pretend, my heart refuses to be fooled.

I'm still struggling to breathe when my phone, which is on an unoccupied seat next to me, lights up. A text has come in.

I give Jared a quick glance, but he's too

engrossed in the movie to notice me watching him. I casually pick up the phone.

I almost choke on my own saliva when I read the message, a few words that pack a big punch.

I'm here. I see you.

I switch it off immediately, but the words ring inside my head like a broken record. They snatch my breath. They make my chest ache.

Jared reaches for my hand and holds it tight. Then he turns to me. Even in the semidarkness I can see the questions on his face. "You're trembling," he says. "Something is wrong, isn't it?"

"I don't...I don't feel well." I swallow hard. "I want to go home."

He doesn't say anything as he releases my hand and pushes out of his chair.

I grab my bag and follow him out of the theater.

The silence between us continues until we get inside the car. Jared leans back his head and closes his eyes, his hands buried in his thick hair. When he opens his eyes again and glances at me, the outrage in them is unmistakable.

"What's going on, Kelsey?" He grinds the words between his teeth.

"I told you I don't feel well." I move my hand up and down my forearm, goosebumps rubbing against my palm. "I have a headache."

"Stop lying to me." He grips the steering wheel so tight the veins on his hand push against his skin. "It's not just about tonight. You've been like this for weeks now."

"I don't know what you mean." Living a lie is hard work. Right now I'm using all my energy to try and hide the truth from him.

"What I mean is, you are always here in person, but your mind is elsewhere. You're so jumpy all the time, even when we're the only two people in the house."

He's referring to an incident that happened yesterday. He walked in on me in the shower. I was so startled that I screamed.

I decide not to respond, afraid to say the wrong thing. Jared is watching me too closely now.

"And you've been cleaning even more than usual. The house is so spotless we could eat off the damn floor."

"It's a habit. My grandmother...she was OCD about cleaning and I guess I inherited it from her. I mentioned it to you once."

The mention of my grandmother makes my stomach swirl with anxiety. Jared doesn't know much about her. I prefer to keep her in the past where she belongs.

Like everyone else, he believes I came from a good family and was raised by a loving grandmother. The truth is, my grandmother was a monster. She punished me for the sins of my mother, who left me on her doorstep when I was a year old. Even though I lived in her house, I took care of myself since I was four. She never cooked so I lived on cereals and stale bread. I washed myself from the kitchen sink with cold water because she forbade me from using hot water, even in the winter. She made me clean the house every day, even when it didn't need it. If she noticed even one speck of dust, I got to feel the consequences of her wrath. It's no wonder that even today, years after she died, I'm still doing the things she had trained me to do. I still clean like a maniac as though she's watching from beyond the grave.

But Jared doesn't know any of those things. He wanted me to be perfect, so I told him a perfect, fake version of my childhood.

"Are you happy, Kelsey?" He stares through the windshield. "Are you happy in our marriage?"

"I am, Jared," I blurt out. "I *am* happy."

"Then act like it." He turns the key in the ignition and drives us home at such a great speed it's a wonder we don't have an accident.

As soon as we're behind closed doors, he goes straight to his office.

CHAPTER 8

I sit inside my car, parked in front of the building that used to be my temporary home when I had nowhere else to go.

The Rosemary Shelter for Women had given me a roof over my head as soon as I arrived in Sanlow. I lived inside the towering building even when I was dating Jared. I never told him about the shelter because I was ashamed.

Jared is working late tonight. Before leaving the house, I sent him a text to tell him I was going to the gym. Another lie that could hurt me. But I was desperate to come to a safe place. Since no men are allowed in the women-only gym, he wouldn't know I went.

The shelter still feels more like home than the fancy house on Montlake Street.

I always return at least once a month, when Jared is out of town, to help out and give back.

I don't tell Jared or anyone else in my new life what I do. They will not understand. Last

Christmas, I suggested to Jared that we should help out at a soup kitchen for a couple of hours. He was horrified. He thought it would be best for us to donate money to such causes instead of getting our hands dirty.

I get out of the car and take a deep breath. Far away from Montlake Street, I can be myself. I can be broken and I can cry freely if I want to.

Behind the doors of the shelter are people who will not judge me, people who do not expect me to be perfect, and one person who knows all my secrets.

It's getting dark and the sun is sinking to the other side of the building. A number of homeless women are entering the wrought iron gate to get dinner and a place to sleep for the night.

Their pain and shame are familiar to me. I recognize the feeling of being lost and having nothing. Whenever I come, I give not only my time, but also money that I steal from the grocery fund.

The dining hall is filled with people from all nationalities, mothers nursing their babies on naked breasts, babies crying for another bite to eat, people slurping soup that trickles down their chins.

I don't look down at any of them. They are my people, my real people.

Rosemary White spots me in the crowd before I see her. She comes to tap me on the shoulder.

"Hello, darling. I didn't know you were coming today." I whirl around and allow myself to be pulled into her warm hug. I stay inside her arms for longer than necessary, inhaling her soothing lavender perfume.

She pulls back and searches my face. "Is everything all right?" Her hand, the one with a scar she never likes to talk about, comes to rest on my cheek.

Her lined face is kind as always and she has the most unusual gray eyes, which are so beautiful they seem unreal. With the gray hair that frames her round face, she looks like an angel. She's my angel. I still remember when she showed up in my life out of the blue, just when I needed her most.

I blink back tears and look deep into her eyes. I can only do that with her. Normally, I keep my gazes brief because I'm afraid my eyes will give me away, that they will reveal the secrets I'm not ready to share with the world.

"I'm not." There's no point in hiding it from her. She knows me too well.

A shadow crosses her features, but it soon disappears and she pats my cheek. "Okay, darling. Help me serve the last people, then we can talk."

I give her a watery smile and follow her to the packed dining hall, where I scoop potato and sausage soup into hard plastic bowls.

Each bowl I serve makes me feel better. There's something about serving others that makes me feel like I'm helping myself.

I allow myself to be in the moment, to realize there are people much worse off than I am.

It's only for a brief moment that I wonder whether Victor has followed me to the shelter. During the drive, I had not noticed anyone behind me. But that doesn't mean he's not out there waiting for me to exit the building so he can continue to make my life hell. It has been a week since he contacted me, but I don't doubt for one second that he'll get in touch again.

I have decided that I won't pay him much attention tonight. This is my home. He can't hurt me here.

A homeless lady with a burn scar on one side of her face comes up to me, two toddlers in her arms. Since she has no free hand to take the bowl, I carry it for her to the nearest table before returning to my station to get soup for the kids as well.

"Thank you," she whispers, looking into my eyes. Her dark eyes are tainted by shame. She's ashamed that she cannot take care of her own kids, that she has to rely on other people for a meal and a bed.

"It's all right." I pat her hand. "We've all been there."

Once everyone is served and the mattresses have been laid out in the sleeping halls, Rosemary comes for me.

She takes me to one of the rooms reserved for the staff and sits me down on the single bed.

"Tell me everything," she says in her husky voice. "I thought you were happy with Jar...your husband. What happened?"

"Something terrible." I wrap a hand around my ponytail.

Rosemary crosses her jean-clad legs and clasps her hands around one knee. "Is your marriage in trouble? You know you can tell me anything."

"That's why I'm here. I don't know who else to talk to." I swallow hard. "I was raped a few weeks ago. The man was my husband's best friend, Victor."

"Goodness." Rosemary inhales sharply, her hand covering her chest, her eyes wild with shock. As soon as she recovers, she pulls me into her arms again. "You poor girl."

"I don't know what to do," I say, choking up.

She lets me go. "The first step is to get it off your chest. You did the right thing coming here to speak to me."

"I went for a run at a lake not too far from our house. Victor showed up out of nowhere. He told me that he knows my secrets."

"You mean—"

I nod. "He knew my real name is not Kelsey."

"And you think he was telling the truth?" Rosemary frowns. "What if he was lying?"

"I wish he were, but I think he does know." I chew the inside of my cheek. "He said he needed an incentive in order to keep his mouth shut. He didn't need to tell me what he wanted. I already knew. He's flirted with me many times."

Rosemary rises from the bed and goes to the door, locking it before coming to sit back down next to me. "What did he do to you, sweetheart?"

"I pushed him away and he attacked me right there in the bushes close to the water."

"What a scumbag." Rosemary places both hands on her cheeks, her skin flushed with anger. "Does your husband know about this?"

"I couldn't tell him, not without telling him everything else about me."

Rosemary reaches for my hand and holds it tight. "He still doesn't know about your past? I thought you wanted to come clean."

I shake my head. "If I tell Jared I was in prison for murder, he'll leave me." As much as he sometimes stifles me by being so controlling, I can't imagine a life without him. "And he might turn me in."

"I understand." Rosemary goes quiet for a long time. "I'm guessing you also didn't report the rape?"

I shake my head.

"So, this Victor is getting away with rape?

What if he attacks you again?"

"There's more." I drop my head into my hands. "He disappeared that night. I hit him with a rock to get him off me, then I just ran home. A few hours later, his wife called my husband to tell him that Victor didn't come home."

"What happened to him?" Rosemary's words are barely audible.

"We still don't know. A few days after his disappearance, he wrote his wife to tell her he needed time away to think about his life. But I think he lied to her."

"I don't understand." The bedsprings sigh as Rosemary shifts.

"I don't think he's gone. Since he left, I've been getting notes and a text message from him." I raise my head again. "He's torturing me from a distance. He reminds me that he knows my secrets."

"But how can he do that when you also have something on him? Isn't he scared that if he exposes you, you might tell the cops what he's done?"

"I don't know." I shrug. "If I do tell the cops, it will be my word against his. I'm in his town. I'm an outsider."

The silence that follows is thick and heavy. We sit side by side, staring at the door, neither of us saying a word.

Rosemary is the first to speak. She lays a hand

on my back, her warmth seeping through my top. "Kelsey, you've been through a lot. I want you to be happy. You deserve to be happy. I think the only way you can do that is by telling your husband everything, even if there's a danger of him leaving you. He might surprise you. He might stay."

"And what if he doesn't? What if he turns me in?"

Rosemary runs a hand through her bob. "You're right. Maybe it's not such a good idea. I wish there were something I could do to help you."

I give her a sad smile. "You've already done enough for me." Talking to her has given me the comfort I had been searching for. "I'll be fine."

Rosemary walks me to my car and waves as I drive away.

On the way home, I notice a black truck trailing behind me for a few minutes. My stomach rolls and sweat starts to trickle down my temples, but I bite down on my lower lip and keep moving forward. I won't let him win.

Instead of driving straight home, I head in the direction of the police station, but before I can reach it, the truck disappears.

Rosemary was right. Victor has as much to lose as I do, maybe even more. If I threaten to expose him, he might leave me alone.

I park in front of the station and pull out my

phone. My fingers hover over the little keys only for a few seconds before I type.

Leave me alone, or I'll tell everyone what you did.

CHAPTER 9

I open my eyes to find the sun spilling into the room through the open windows. Both Jared and I have always preferred not to close the blinds at night. We love seeing the stars.

I hate that the new bars at the bedroom window disturb the view, but Jared says one can't be too careful. He had them installed only recently.

I glance at him. He's still sleeping, his mouth slightly open, his eyelashes gently brushing the area underneath his eyes. I once told him that for a man, he has the longest eyelashes I have ever seen.

Today is a good day, at least I hope it is. Despite seeing the black truck two days ago, I haven't heard from Victor. He's still hiding out there in the shadows and it's only a matter of time before he emerges again to taunt me. But for now, I can breathe.

As I watch Jared, he suddenly stirs. Seconds

later, he opens his eyes. "Hey, wifey," he says, pulling me close. He has been kinder to me lately.

"Hey, husband." I hold on tight, enjoying every second in the circle of his arms. I don't know how long it will be until it's over.

Eventually, it *will* be over. I have a feeling it will not end well.

Jared pulls away and studies my face, as though learning it for the first time, memorizing it. The only truth about me is my looks. If only he could see beneath my skin, he would not like what he finds.

"You don't remember, do you?" he asks with a grin.

"Remember what?" I hold my breath as I wait for him to respond.

"Your birthday, silly." He kisses the tip of my nose. "How can you not remember your own birthday?"

"I don't know. It's never been that important to me."

July 12th is not a day I like to celebrate. Why would I celebrate the day I was brought into the world by a woman who did not want me? Why would I celebrate the day that started the chain of events that made my life hell? I prefer to forget.

"Well, it's important to me," he says, his voice still thick with sleep. "I bless the day you were born." He reaches underneath his pillow and comes out holding a black velvet box.

I pretend to be excited as I sit up in bed and snap it open, gasping when my gaze lands on a fragile diamond necklace that rests on a bed of silk. "It's beautiful." I pick up the diamond and the fragile silver chain dangles underneath it like a thin stream of water.

"Just like you," he says, pulling me back underneath the covers. "Do I get a thank you?"

I giggle and place the necklace back in its box. I kiss him hard on the lips.

We spend the entire morning in bed, and that's where he serves me breakfast. As he pours attention on me, I do my best to enjoy my time with him.

"How about we go for a walk at the lake before we head to lunch?" Jared asks when we're taking a shower together, getting ready for the day. "It looks wonderful outside."

I hesitate before responding, pretending to be focused on slathering my arm with soap.

"So, are you up for it?" he asks.

"Yeah, let's do it."

I haven't been to the lake since the night we went searching for Victor. I have only been watching it from a distance, yearning to go to the water, but terrified of the memories.

"By the way," Jared says when we're getting dressed. "Why don't you go jogging anymore?"

"I don't know. I'm taking a break."

"But it's been over a month? You used to jog every weekend." He comes to put his arms around me. "Is it because of what happened to Victor?"

I rub the back of my neck. "What do you mean?"

He kisses the side of my neck. "He disappeared after going jogging at the lake."

"Yes. But he didn't actually disappear. He left town."

Jared releases me so he can finish dressing in white-washed jeans and a black t-shirt. "Yeah, but when we all thought he had disappeared...that gave a lot of people a scare. It shook the community. That's why I had the bars installed. You never know these days. Victor is safe wherever he is, but it could have ended differently."

"You're right," I say and leave it at that.

Five minutes later, we step out the door and walk hand in hand down the path leading to the lake.

Things have changed. Before the rape, when I walked down the path I saw only beauty. Now all I see are the dead shrubs and wildflowers that frame it. I can even smell the rotting undergrowth.

I'm relieved when we don't walk all the way to the place where it happened. Since it's quite a distance away, we decide to sit on the sand and admire the water. I'm glad for a chance to rest because my head is starting to spin.

We sit next to each other in silence, enjoying the calm before my storm. When Jared finally suggests that we should return home because it looks as though it might rain, I get to my feet so fast my head spins.

"I love you," he says when we're back indoors. "I'm sorry I haven't said that to you in a while. I've been so busy with work and everything."

"You don't have to say the words for me to know." I follow him into the living room.

Then out of nowhere, the sound of someone coughing makes me jump, then people start emerging from behind furniture.

"Surprise," they all shout. "Happy birthday, Kelsey."

Now I understand why Jared took me to the lake.

Before I can recover from the sudden surprise, they all start singing. Instead of feeling excited and honored, I'm stressed and anxious. Even though I'm smiling, pretending to be touched, the one thing I want to do is run.

I have been avoiding all of them, especially Rachel, who is now back in town. I'm finding it hard to be around her knowing what her husband did to me and being unable to tell her.

I wish I could tell her that instead of grieving his departure, she should be glad he's gone. She's better off without him. I'm actually glad she's not among the women in the room.

Everything happens fast after that. I'm greeted, hugged, and kissed by women who are still strangers to me. They sit me down to enjoy my party while Jared gives me a wink and excuses himself.

"We'll celebrate alone later. Spend time with your friends."

I scan the faces of the women around me. As much as they don't know me, I don't know them.

I invite them to my house. I feed them. We exchange pleasantries. But none of them are my friends. How could they be my friends if they don't know who I am? But what does that mean for Jared and me? Can I call him my husband?

"We brought cupcakes," Linda shouts, her shrill voice grating my ears.

As the ladies launch into their latest escapades, show off their recent jewelry purchases, and complain about their husbands, I glance discreetly at the time on my phone, wondering when they will leave.

"We miss your dinner parties, Kelsey," Connie says, dabbing her lips with a pink napkin.

"I'm sorry." I lift a cocktail glass to my lips. "I've been so busy with other things lately."

"Well, maybe the next dinner should be at our place," Connie continues. "I'm not the best cook, but I'll do my best."

"By the way, do you know what's going on with Rachel?" Linda asks me. "I mean she was here, but she had to leave because of a headache."

"Okay." I frown at her. "But I don't understand. What do you mean what's going on with her?" We all know what's going on.

"Since Victor left her, she has completely withdrawn from everyone. I invited her to my place a couple of times, but she always cancels at the last minute."

"That's no surprise," a blonde woman I don't recognize adds. "I'd probably do the same thing. How embarrassing would it be to have your husband leave you out of the blue?"

Connie leans toward me and whispers. "Do you think Victor has left her for good?"

I shake my head. "I don't know."

"Oh." She sounds disappointed. "I thought you would know since your husband is his best friend. He must have said something to him."

"I haven't heard anything." I take a sip of my piña colada.

It suddenly dawns on me why they're here. It has nothing to do with celebrating my birthday. I probably don't even matter to them. They came because they're looking for gossip. They want something to spread across town.

I have to be careful what I say to them or anyone else. If I say the wrong thing, I'm the one who could end up getting hurt.

It doesn't surprise me that thirty minutes after getting nothing from me, they take their fancy cupcake containers and leave. They wasted their time.

As soon as I close the door, I lean against it and exhale. When the knot in my stomach unravels, I return to the living room to clean up.

That's when I come across another note tucked behind one of the couch cushions.

I snatch it up before Jared walks into the room, push it into my jeans pocket and read it in the downstairs bathroom.

Happy birthday! Expect more surprises from me.

CHAPTER 10

I sit up in bed and search the darkness. I dreamed he was in the room watching me sleep. But it's not possible. I would have heard the door being opened. He also wouldn't be able to get through the bars at the windows.

Everything is fine, undisturbed. The only sound in the room is that of Jared snoring gently.

I pick up my phone to check the time. It's close to 1:00 a.m.

I hate the nightmares that yank me from sleep almost every night. I don't even remember the last time I had a full night's rest.

I sit in bed for a while, afraid that if I get out, Jared will hear me.

After he revealed to me that he knows I clean at night, I stopped. I still wake up night after night, but I remain in bed.

Since my birthday a week ago, Jared has been even nicer and less controlling. Last weekend, we even went to church and he allowed me to choose my own outfit.

I cannot make him suspicious again.

While he sleeps, the cloak of darkness wraps itself around me, suffocating me as I gaze at the windows.

It's been so hot this summer that we keep them open through the night. For the first time, I'm grateful for the bars, even though sometimes they remind me of the prison cell in which I spent ten years of my life.

I clasp my hands tightly in my lap and force myself to think of less painful memories. The only thing that comes to mind is my wedding with Jared, a quick ceremony in Vegas.

He had wanted a big wedding, with all his friends present, but when we visited Vegas a week after we were engaged, I talked him into getting married there instead. Being on the run, I didn't want anyone paying me any attention, except Jared.

Since he also didn't have family members he could invite to the wedding, I guess it was an easy decision. That night in Vegas, we gave each other the gift of family.

If only I could say we lived happily ever after.

I push aside the memories. It's killing me to sit in bed doing nothing. Trying to harness my fears is torture.

Careful not to wake Jared, I slide out of bed. I make it to the door and open it without him stirring. I'd feel so guilty if he wakes up. He got home late from work.

Unlike many times I woke up at night in the past, tonight I don't reach for a rag or a broom. Instead, I head downstairs for something to drink. There's nothing wrong with that. A cup of rooibos tea might help soothe my nerves.

When I come to the kitchen door my blood goes cold. The small, red light on the kettle is on and it's piercing through the darkness.

The first thought that drops into my mind is that I should run. But a part of me is tired of doing that. My teeth are gritted as I fumble along the wall where the light switch should be and flick it on, hoping what I'm seeing is my imagination.

My hopes are quickly dashed. The kettle is switched on and it's boiling now.

I switch it off. My thirst for tea has dissipated. I bite back a scream when I notice a note peeking from underneath the kettle. Fear snakes through my heart.

The countdown has started. Leave this town or you'll regret it.

It takes a while for the words to register in my mind. He wants me gone. He wanted me gone all along. I'm sure it's because he's afraid I'll report him to the cops.

For Victor to come into our home even when Jared is in goes to show how dangerous he is.

The doors and windows are locked. How does he get into our house? Did Jared give him a key for emergencies?

Unable to hold myself upright any longer, I shuffle to the kitchen table and drop into a chair. My throat aches to scream out my frustration. But I can't.

Jared can't find out. I have no choice but to suffer in silence.

A strange sound makes me sit up straight.

My frantic gaze moves to the window in time to spot a dark figure moving on the other side of the glass only moments before it steps back into the night, merging with the darkness.

It's him. It has to be.

I jump out of the chair so fast I almost send it crashing to the floor. I catch it in time, then I rush to the window, knowing it might be foolish to do so. He could have a gun. He could shoot me straight through the glass.

But I have nothing to worry about. He's running to the gate, gone for now. But how far will he go to drive me out of town?

Weak with fear, I fall back into my chair, my gaze still fixed on the window.

"You have to stop this," someone says from behind me. I turn around to see Jared standing there, his hair ruffled by sleep. "You have to stop waking up in the middle of the night."

"I'm sorry." I tighten my fingers around the note in my hand. "I didn't mean to wake you." Thank God he didn't come a few minutes earlier. He would have seen the note. He would have seen Victor on our property.

"You didn't wake me. I got up to go to the bathroom and found you missing from the bed. Have you been cleaning again?" He moves to the kettle, turns it on, and removes a yellow mug from the cabinet above it. He must be so sleepy he doesn't notice the steam rising from the opening.

"I felt like a cup of tea," I lie.

"Sweetheart, this is not normal. You should be sleeping like a normal person."

"Maybe I'm not normal." I chuckle in spite of myself.

He leans against the sink and watches me for a while, his arms crossed. "Maybe you need to go on sleep medication. You hardly sleep."

"You know I don't like meds, unless I have to take them." There's no way I'll take sleeping pills. How will I be able to protect myself when I'm knocked out?

"But, sweetheart, your body needs to return to functioning normally."

He turns around and pours each of us a cup of tea. He drinks his while gazing out the window. When he turns back to me, his brows are knitted.

"What's the matter?" I ask, blowing over the surface of the hot liquid, sending steam streaming away from me. "You look like you saw a ghost."

It's hard to act normal when I'm terrified out of my mind. What if Victor is back out there? What if he's ready to tell Jared everything about me?

"Did we leave the gate open before bed?" He looks back out the window. "I remember closing it. I always do."

My nerves tense immediately. "It's open?" I push myself to my feet and walk to where he's standing.

It's true. Victor did not close the gate. I don't know whether it was done on purpose or because he was in a hurry to get away. "That's strange," I murmur.

"Yes, it is," Jared says. "I'll go and close it. I'll be right back."

I watch him through the window as he closes the gate, wondering how long it will be until he puts two and two together. I'm actually surprised that I've been able to keep the truth from him for so long. But I'm also shocked that Victor has not exposed me yet.

When I'm in bed again after two cups of tea, I try to fall sleep, but I don't succeed. I can't forget what happened downstairs before Jared walked into the kitchen.

He goes back to sleep almost immediately. I'm a bit envious of his ability to nod off so easily.

I wish I knew how it feels to be normal, to live a life that's not driven by fear.

CHAPTER 11

In the middle of dinner, Jared gets an emergency call from the station. As I watch his car drive off, my heart sinks.

Lately, I've been feeling much safer with him around. After Victor's last note a week ago, I've constantly been on pins and needles.

He ordered me to leave town. I disobeyed. What will he do next? How will he punish me?

I shut the doors and windows and go to the bathroom upstairs. As much as I wanted Jared to stay home with me, there's something I've been wanting to do, something he cannot know about.

Holding my breath, I reach into the cabinet underneath the sink until my fingers find the slim box I hid there. I take it with me to the toilet.

My heartbeat thrashes in my ears as I tear it open and pull out the pregnancy test.

Feeling sick has become a familiar sensation in my body. At first, I thought it was brought on by the stress of everything that's going on, but last weekend, it occurred to me that I had missed a period.

Alarm bells went off immediately. I never miss a period. There can only be one terrifying explanation.

I bought the test online the day after the last note, but I didn't have the courage to find out the truth. Until now.

I pee on the stick before I change my mind. The idea of being pregnant makes me want to throw up, but there's no use burying my head in the sand.

I sit on the tiled floor with my arms around my knees, waiting for the test to spit out the results.

The wait should only be five minutes, but it feels like hours. Since there's no clock in the bathroom and I forgot my phone in the room, I count my heart beats.

One. Two. Three.

Instead of counting exactly three hundred heartbeats, I count three hundred. The results should be ready.

I cannot bring myself to look, but I have to.

I reach for the stick and stare at it through my blurry vision. There are tears in my eyes. I didn't even know I was crying. I wipe them away and peer at the little window displaying the results.

Two pink lines.

A jagged roar erupts in the room and bounces off the wall. It takes a few seconds for me to realize it's coming from me.

To keep myself sane in prison, I stayed in my mind, where I created the reality that made me happy. I saw images of me laughing with a handsome husband next to me and our kids playing around us.

Now it's happening. I'm pregnant with a miracle. But it's all wrong. Jared had made it clear from the start, before we even got married, that he doesn't want kids. I loved him so much that I agreed. A week after we got married, I brought up the topic again. He shut me down so harshly that the subject never crossed my lips again. Determined to prove how serious he was, a few days later, he had himself snipped and only told me after the fact.

Left with no other choice but to accept a future without children, I made myself believe it's best for me not to bring a kid into a damaged world. The child might end up as damaged as I am. I also didn't want to have to lie to my child about who I am.

Now this.

I wrap an arm around my stomach as more tears flood my eyes. This baby is both a miracle and a complication.

The child growing inside me can only be Victor's.

He or she will remind me every day of what happened to me in the bushes by the lake.

I remain on the floor for at least an hour, too weak to get up, unable to stop crying.

When I finally run out of tears, my head is pounding.

I can't tell Jared yet, but I need to speak to someone. I run out to throw the stick in the dumpster, then I run back inside, panting with fear. Inside the bedroom, I grab my phone and call Rosemary. She doesn't answer the call, but seven minutes after I hang up, she calls back. When she hears my tear-smothered voice, she knows something is wrong.

"What happened, darling?"

"I'm scared," I say, pulling the comforter over my body. I'm a full-grown woman with a baby in my belly, but right now I feel like a helpless child.

It's selfish of me to disturb Rosemary at night, but she's the only person I can trust. She has always been like a mother to me.

"Kelsey, tell me what happened," she says in a hoarse whisper.

"I'm pregnant," I say before I change my mind.

Silence plugs the line. Before it stretches on for too long, I speak, "I don't know what to do."

Rosemary clears her throat. "And you think it's—"

"I'm one hundred percent sure." I pinch the

bridge of my nose. I can't even pretend it's Jared's kid.

"What a mess," Rosemary says. "I can only imagine how you must feel."

"I don't even know how I feel right now. Broken, I guess."

Rosemary lets out an audible breath. "Sweetheart, this is a tough question to ask you, but do you want to keep the baby?"

"I haven't thought about that yet. I just found out about the pregnancy." I still can't believe there's a baby growing inside of me.

The clock is ticking. I have to make decisions. I have to make them fast. As much as I can't bear the thought of giving birth to Victor's child, it's an innocent baby.

But what if I keep it? What would that do to my marriage? How would it impact my life?

"I understand," Rosemary says. "Come to the shelter tomorrow so we can talk more about this. It's a huge burden to carry on your own."

"Yeah. I'd like that." I'm not even thinking of going for an hour or two. It might be best for me to hide out at the shelter for a few days, to give myself time to come to terms with what's happening. If I have to tell Jared about the pregnancy, I need to prepare myself.

"Do you mind if I stay for like two or three days?" I ask Rosemary. "I'll help out."

"Of course, I don't mind. It's your home. You

can come any day and stay for as long as you want. I think it's a good idea. You should take a few days away from your husband to think about what you want to do next. I'll spend those nights at the shelter with you."

Rosemary has a home to go to, but sometimes she chooses to spend the night among the women she helps.

As soon as I hang up the phone, I call Jared, wondering if he'll let me go. He doesn't answer. He calls back half an hour later.

"Missing me already?" he asks.

"I need to get away for a few days," I say, crossing my fingers as I used to do as a child.

"To get away?" His tone hardens. "Why? Where are you going?"

"I want to visit a friend in Polson. She's sick. I need...I want to be there for her."

"I didn't know you had a close friend in Polson. Who is she?"

"Mandy. We went to school together." I close my eyes. "We had lost touch for a while. She's sick."

If he finds out I'm lying, there will be hell to pay. But I have no other choice. If he sees me in the state I'm in, he will demand to know what's wrong.

"What kind of sickness does she have?" Suspicion deepens his voice.

"Cancer," I say without thinking. "She has

breast cancer."

After a long silence, he clears his throat. "Fine. Go to your friend. When do you want to leave?"

"I...I think I should leave right away."

"In the middle of the night? Why not wait till morning?" The old, controlling Jared is back. I can tell because his tone has suddenly gone cold. "I can drive you."

"No." I shake my head. "You're busy. I'll drive myself. She needs me, Jared. I need to go right away. I'll be back in three days."

"Make sure it's three days and no more than that." He hangs up.

CHAPTER 12

I arrive at the gates of the Rosemary Shelter shortly before 10:00 p.m.

As soon as I had packed a small bag and put it in the car, Jared called again. When I picked up the phone, he hung up.

He was clearly telling me without words that he did not approve of me going away without him. It would be hard for him to control me from a distance.

As soon as I get out of the car, Rosemary rushes out to receive me.

I melt into her loving arms, the urge to cry so overwhelming, but the tears refuse to come. I'm completely numb right now, both physically and mentally.

During the short drive, I tried hard not to think about the pregnancy. With my emotions raging out of control, I would not have been able to drive safely.

Rosemary takes my arm and leads me inside,

where most of the residents are already asleep. She takes me to one of the empty rooms and sits me down.

"I don't think I can get rid of this baby," I say before she even says a word. "I don't think I'll be able to live with myself."

"It's your decision." She places a hand on top of mine. "But you do know that this changes everything, right? You might have to tell your husband about the rape. You're slim, but eventually the pregnancy will show."

"I'm scared. As soon as I tell him, he'll know it's not his child." I bury my hands in my hair. "Jared can't have kids. He never wanted them. Not long after we got married, he had a vasectomy."

"Wow." Rosemary's shoulders slump under the weight of my problems. "He really doesn't want kids, does he?" She sits up straight again. "Kelsey, you seem to be terrified of your husband. Has he hurt you?"

Even though Rosemary knows about my past secrets, I have never confided in her about Jared. I never told her how controlling he is and how sometimes I'm scared of him.

"No," I say. "Not physically. He does have a temper, but he locks himself away until it passes."

"How do you think he'll handle this?"

"I don't know." I lay a hand on my stomach.

"I don't think he will take it well." That's an understatement. Every time I think of telling Jared about the baby and the rape, I shiver with dread. "If I didn't go behind his back that night, I wouldn't be dealing with this."

"What do you mean?" Rosemary asks.

"The night it happened, I told him I was going to the gym, but I changed my mind at the last minute. It was so lovely outside that I decided to go for a run at the lake instead. He hates it when I jog at night. I didn't tell him I was going." My chin hits my chest. "He might blame this on me."

Rosemary grabs me by the shoulders and turns me to face her. "It's not your fault, Kelsey. You have to understand that. You just happened to come across a sick man. That monster is to blame, not you."

A tear trickles down my cheek. "Thank you, Rosemary." I wipe the tear away with the back of my hand. "I'm tired. Do you mind if I go to sleep now? We can talk in the morning."

"No, I don't mind. You should get some rest. You're safe here." She kisses my cheek. "And I'm here to support you in whatever decision you make. No woman should have to go through something like this alone."

"I appreciate you," I say to her as she moves to the door.

She hesitates before turning around with a sad smile. "I'm sorry I can't do more for you."

"You've done more for me than anyone ever has. You showed me that there's another way. You gave me a home when I had nowhere else to go. Now you're helping me sort out my mess."

"I didn't have a choice," she says softly. She told me once that when she sees a broken soul, it's hard for her to turn her back.

When she leaves, I lock the door. My gaze takes in the small room. It's not much bigger than my prison cell used to be, but at least it has walls and a big enough window to enable me to see a large portion of the sky. I'm glad it's not too big that someone can fit through it. There's a great chance that Victor has followed me here.

I sink onto the small bed, my hands around my belly. I force myself into feeling nothing, pretending that I'm not pregnant at all. But my mind is not a fool.

Trying to harness my emotions, I close my eyes and focus on the silence in the room.

When my phone rings, I cringe. Jared's name flashes on the screen. I consider not answering the call, but I hate not knowing what the consequences will be.

"Why did it take you so long to get to the phone?" he asks, his tone still cold.

I ache to know that the man who has been so sweet to me the past few days is gone. Jared is showing his true colors again.

"Sorry," I say. "I couldn't find it inside my

bag." It's a stupid lie, but it's the best I can do.

"Are you still driving?" he asks.

Panic wells up inside my throat, but I pull myself together. "Yes." There's no way I can tell him that I've already arrived. He would know immediately that I'm lying. "I should be there in about an hour."

I hope he can't hear the silence in the room. What if he's listening for sounds of cars? Then again, it's late at night and it's normal for the roads to be quiet.

"Call me when you get there."

I tell him I will. When I'm about to hang up the phone, he calls my name.

"Yes," I answer.

"You *will* come back after three days, won't you?" There's a silent threat in the spaces between the words. He's daring me to give the wrong answer.

"Of course. I'll come back home." I massage my left temple with my free hand. "Are you afraid I might leave you like Victor left Rachel?"

"Maybe. Sometimes people can be unpredictable. They do things we don't expect them to. I need you to promise that you won't do anything stupid."

"Like what?" I bite my lower lip.

"Never mind. Drive safely. I need to go."

My hands are shaking as I hang up the phone and fall back against the single pillow on the bed.

An uncomfortable thought drops into my mind. What if Jared knows?

Before I can obsess over the thought, my phone pings as a new text arrives. It's from my stalker.

Your time is almost up. Leave town or face the consequences.

His words leave me cold as they always do. Now that I'm pregnant, I'm even more terrified. What will he do if he finds out about the baby?

A rush of adrenaline shoots through me and I get back to my feet.

I can't do this. I can't allow him to have so much power over me.

Even though I'm scared of Jared's reaction, the only way to release Victor's grip on me is to come clean.

Still high on adrenaline, I grab my bag and open the door. I won't bother Rosemary again with my problems tonight. She's probably already settled in bed. I'll send her a text on the way home.

When I reach the front door of the shelter and turn the key in the lock, she calls my name.

She's standing behind me in a faded blue nightgown that reaches her ankles.

As I watch her confused face, guilt stabs me in the chest.

"Where are you going?" she asks.

"I can't stay here. It was a mistake. You were right. I should tell Jared what happened. It's the only way I can free myself."

"Are you sure you don't want to sleep on it?"

"I've slept on it for a long time now." I draw in a deep breath. "Thank you for everything you've done for me. I can't bother you with this anymore. What happened is not my fault, but I'm guilty for keeping it from my husband. He deserves to know."

Victor has made enough threats. It's time I take action.

"I think that's a good idea." Rosemary comes to give me a hug and we say our goodbyes.

My confidence only takes me as far as my car, where I find a sharp knife waiting for me on the driver's seat.

CHAPTER 13

I hand a homeless woman a jam and peanut butter sandwich. She thanks me with a toothless grin.

I haven't changed my mind about telling Jared everything, but I couldn't do it last night. After finding the knife inside my car, I was too much in shock to drive.

Rosemary had been standing at the door, watching me enter the car, when she heard me scream. She insisted I spend the night and return home in the morning.

Even though she got rid of the knife, I saw it the entire night behind my eyelids, lying there on my seat, a dangerous message from Victor. A line has been crossed. The game he's playing has turned deadly.

As I help serve the rest of the breakfast, I rehearse inside my head all the things I want to say to Jared.

"What if I'm making a mistake?" I ask

Rosemary for the third time today. "What if he turns me in?"

"If he loves you, he won't." Rosemary pours fruit tea into a plastic mug and offers it to one of the residents.

"What if he doesn't love me enough?" I've been turning the question over and over in my mind since last night. What if Jared decides he doesn't love me enough to protect me?

"Then he wasn't meant to be yours." Rosemary's shoulders rise and sink as she takes a breath. "I think you're right to want to tell him. What other options do you have?"

"Not many." I've also been thinking of what I'd do if Jared is not on my side. I can either run or turn myself in. I'm not a murderer. I never killed my grandmother. But what I did wrong was run from the law.

I still remember that night, the night I was beaten up by my cellmate and was driven to a nearby hospital for treatment. I still remember the sound of screaming rubber as the police van swerved off the road to avoid an oncoming truck. I had not planned for that accident, but I survived it with only a broken arm. The two guards did not make it. As I stood on the side of the road, bleeding from new and old wounds, I couldn't resist the temptation of fleeing, running toward my freedom. But now it looks as though I have hit a dead end.

I hate the idea of returning to prison, but am I strong enough to run again, especially while pregnant? It's no longer just about me. It's about the baby, the baby I have thought about all night. I have to be prepared to raise it alone because Jared might not be on board. I won't blame him.

It's a lot for any man to deal with. Knowing that his friend raped me might be too much for him to handle. But I made a decision last night. I'm not getting rid of the baby. Even my mother, who I had considered to be heartless for leaving me behind, still brought me into the world, even though she didn't want me.

"You can do this." Rosemary places an arm around my shoulders. "You're stronger than you give yourself credit for. You have gone through so much in your life and you're still standing. Whatever comes your way, you'll be able to handle it."

I hand over my last sandwich and turn to her. "Wish me luck," I say.

Fifteen minutes later, we're both standing outside and I'm thanking her again for everything she has done for me. There's no guarantee that I will ever see her again as a free woman. I might end up behind bars by the end of the day.

There are tears in Rosemary's eyes as she takes both my hands in hers. "What if you don't do it?" she says suddenly.

I shake my head. "What? What do you mean?"

"What if you only tell your husband about the rape and the baby and leave your past out of it?" She inhales sharply. "That way you don't have to worry that he'll call the cops on you."

My shoulders sink. "I considered that option, but it won't work. As soon as he finds out that it's Victor who raped me, he might go searching for him. What if he finds him and confronts him? I'm pretty sure Victor will tell him everything about me." I lean against my car. "I think it's better I tell him. I'm tired, Rosemary. I'm tired of keeping secrets." Maybe going to prison might actually be a relief. I will no longer have to run. Having to constantly come up with lies to hide my secrets is exhausting.

"Maybe you're right." Rosemary blinks away tears. "I don't want you to get hurt, that's all. I'm terrified for you."

"You're so sweet to try and find ways to help me, but there's no way out. I have to go through the eye of the storm." I give her a quick hug and pull open the car door.

She continues to watch me until I drive through the gate.

When the shelter becomes a dot in the distance, tears spring into my eyes.

My vision is so clouded that I worry I might cause an accident. I don't even bother to wipe them away because they're coming way too fast.

I drive slowly, afraid to reach home, to come face-to-face with my fears. Jared will be surprised to see me back after only one night. As far as he's concerned, I'm still out of town.

When I reach the center of town, I slow down even more and watch people living their lives, rushing to work or other places, running errands. Some of them have their own problems, but I'm pretty sure they're nothing compared to mine.

When I drive past the police station, something inside me shifts and fear grabs me by the throat.

I can't do it.

Without thinking about what I'm doing, I turn the car around and drive in the direction that leads out of town. My hands are tight on the steering wheel, my heart frozen inside my chest.

As memories of prison flood my mind, it occurs to me that the only right thing for me to do is run. I've done it before. I managed to create a new life. I can do it again. I can create another life for me and the baby.

I drive for over an hour, only stopping to withdraw cash from an ATM.

This time, I make it to Polson and pull up in front of a small motel. I pay for one night, but I'm not even sure I'll stay that long. I just need to slow down, to come up with a plan.

Inside the room, I give Rosemary a call.

"Have you told him?" she asks, hopeful.

"No." I massage my left temple. "I didn't go home."

"You didn't? Why?"

"I needed to get out of Sanlow." I pick up the pillow and hug it to my body for comfort. "I'm not coming back."

"But I thought—"

"Yeah, me too. I thought I was brave enough to face Jared. But I'm not. I'm also not brave enough to return to prison. I don't think I'd be able to survive it a second time."

"What will you do now? Where are you?"

"I'm in Polson...in a motel." I let out a breath. "I'm calling to say goodbye. I'll never forget what you did for me."

"Kelsey, you can't leave. You never know how your husband might have reacted. He could have protected you."

"Maybe. But there's no guarantee. I can't take the risk. I have a baby to protect."

Even though Rosemary continues to try to talk me into returning to Sanlow, I stand my ground. She offers me money to help me start over, but I refuse. I can't ask more of her. At least I have the four hundred dollars I withdrew from our household account. I only hope Jared will not notice until a few days later. Or maybe he won't care. He knows I'm out of town. It would be normal for me to need money.

He will be devastated when he finds out I'm gone, but I'm not only doing this for me and the baby. I'm also doing it for him. If I tell him the truth about myself and he decides to protect me, he would be breaking the law by harboring a fugitive. I don't want us both to end up behind bars.

The one good thing about running is that Victor will finally get what he wants and leave me alone. In a way, I'll be free.

I curl up on the bed and wrap my arms around my stomach, breathing in and out through my mouth. When I find my strength again, I pull out my phone and go online to research places that are easy to get lost in.

This time, I'll choose a big city, where people don't care about my business. I'll be a regular single mom raising her baby on her own.

CHAPTER 14

Shortly after 3:00 p.m., I'm eating a sandwich I bought in the snack machine of the motel, when I get another call from Jared.

He already called several times, but I ignored all his calls. The smart thing to do would have been to get rid of the phone hours ago, but I couldn't get myself to do it. It's a big step toward cutting myself off from the life I have created.

I plan to leave the motel tonight and I will leave the phone behind, but right now I'm not ready. I continue to stare at the screen, tears rolling down my cheeks. It's hard to let go of him, of us. To make it easier, I remind myself that our marriage is imperfect. Jared is far from perfect. Without him in my life, I have more freedom. I'll be able to make my own choices, to go where I want and dress how I like without his approval.

The phone stops ringing. A text message comes in. For a moment, I fear it's Victor, but it's Jared.

Baby, where are you? I've been trying to reach you all day. Call me.

I pick up the phone and press it to my chest, just as a wave of nausea hits me. The phone drops to the stained carpet and I rush to the bathroom. After throwing up, I study the mildew and broken tiles. Even though my marriage to Jared wasn't a fairytale, I had a nice home. I never had to worry about not having enough to eat.

When I return to the bedroom, it hits me that starting over might not be as easy as I think it is. Last time I was alone, and now I have a baby to take care of.

Another text comes in as I dry my lips with a rough towel. This time it's Victor.

Adios. Don't ever return.

I crumple to the floor next to the phone, weak with relief. It's over. I never have to worry about Victor hurting me again. I only hope that he will not follow me into my new life. But I doubt it. As long as I'm away from Sanlow, I won't be a danger to him. Maybe he'll even return home to Rachel. I can't help feeling sorry for the woman. But she's no longer my problem.

The phone starts to ring again, another call from Jared. This time, I can't resist. In order to move forward, I need closure.

I press the phone to my ear and wait for him to speak.

"Kelsey," he says, his tone like gravel. "Where the hell are you, and why haven't you been answering my calls?"

"Because I need to go away." I drag myself to the bed and close my eyes.

"What are you talking about? You *are* away."

"I'm not coming back, Jared. I just want to say goodbye. I love you, but it was not meant to be."

"Is this a sick joke?" His voice is edged with steel. "What do you think you're doing?"

"I don't know yet. But I can't come back to Sanlow. I can't come back to you." I push a hand through my hair. "I'm sorry."

"Sweetheart, don't be stupid. Whatever it is, whatever you're going through, we can work through it together. Come home. I love you."

"I love you too, Jared. But I'm not the person you think I am."

"Of course, I do." His sharp tone makes me jump. "You are my wife, the woman I love. I'm aware that you've been going through stuff. I saw in your eyes that you were struggling with something. Whatever it is, let me help you. We are married, for God's sake."

I let out a bitter laugh. "It's not as simple as

that. If you knew who I am, you would hate me."

"I could never hate you. Never in a million years. I love you too much." He lowers his voice. "Kelsey, you have to come home. This is where you belong."

Instead of responding, I move the phone from my ear and switch it off. Answering his call was a mistake. I could never make him understand why I have to leave him, not without opening up about my past.

Talking to him did give me some kind of closure. Now it's time to move on, to start again.

Picking up my bag and the small notebook on which I jotted down details of my next life, I look around the room for the last time.

As soon as I pull the door open, I jump back in surprise, a scream stuck inside my throat.

"Ja...Jared."

"It's me, my love." He pulls me into his arms. "Thank God you're all right," he whispers into my hair. "I was worried out of my mind."

He breaks the embrace and cups my face with his hands, lowers his lips to mine. I'm too weak with shock to do anything as thoughts scramble for space inside my head.

"Don't look so scared, baby. It's me, your husband. I'm here to save you from making a mistake." He lifts my bag from the floor.

I slump against the wall, faint with shock. "How did you—"

"How did I find you?" He draws in a deep breath. "You've been acting strange for a couple of weeks now so I put a tracker on your car. I needed to know where you are at all times to make sure you're safe."

My mouth opens and closes like that of a fish gasping for air. When he closes the distance between us, I flinch.

He sighs as he tucks a strand of hair behind my ear like he always does. "You're a mess. We need to go home so you can clean up. You're my perfect wife, remember?"

"I'm not coming back with you, Jared."

"Would you rather go to prison?" He cocks an eyebrow. "That's right, baby, I know your not-so-little secret."

His words feel like a punch in my face. It takes a few seconds for me to recover from his revelation. I want to tell him I don't believe him, but I seem to have lost my ability to speak.

"It's all right. You don't need to say anything." He runs a fingertip down my cheek. "I'm not here to hurt you. I came to take you home where you're safe. I'm on your side here. Do you understand what I'm saying, Kelsey?" I give an involuntary nod. "You will walk out of this dirty motel and go home with me so I can protect you. If you refuse, I'll call the cops right now. Your choice."

I'm still too shaken to respond, so he chooses

for me. He takes my hand, squeezing tight, and walks me to a red Toyota. When we pass the reception desk, he greets the man behind the counter like an old friend.

"We enjoyed a good game of chess while I waited for you to come to your senses," Jared says, opening the car door for me.

Whistling, he gets behind the wheel and drives me back to Sanlow. I don't fight him because something about him sends a chill down my spine.

What if it was him? What if he was my stalker and not Victor? But it doesn't make sense. Victor wants me gone while Jared wants me to stay.

The truth is, I'm terrified of starting again, running into the unknown where other dangers could be awaiting me. But how will Victor react to my return?

"Everything will be great from now on. As long as you behave, I will do my duty as a husband to protect you. But you have to promise to never do something as stupid as running away again."

I stare out the window, saying nothing until we get home. Inside, he takes me to the living room and tells me to sit.

"Let's talk," he says, pulling up a chair so we're facing each other. He places a hand on my cheek. "Is there anything else you're keeping from me?"

"I'm pregnant." My chin hits my chest. I need to tell him now before he finds out on his own. I'm surprised he hasn't already noticed that my stomach has started to swell a bit. Or maybe he already knows and was giving me a chance to come forward. After today, I'll never underestimate him again.

When his hand drops from my cheek, I look up into his eyes. His face is puce with anger, veins popping through the skin on his forehead. I've seen him angry before, but not like this. This is the version of himself he normally brings out inside his office.

Was it a mistake telling him? What choice did I have?

"It's not mine," he finally says.

"Yes, it's not." I struggle to my feet and shuffle to the window, afraid he might strike me. "I was raped."

A sharp intake of breath fills the silence. Then something crashes against the wall. The sound makes me jump, but I don't turn. I'm afraid of what I'll see on his face. I clench my fists tightly at my sides, waiting for the storm to pass.

Finally, he approaches me, coming to stand behind me, but not touching my body. I can feel his warmth and his breath at the back of my neck, but he doesn't say a word.

I turn around slowly and meet his eyes. "You don't want kids and I get that, but I didn't plan this." I'm fully prepared for him to drive me out of his life.

"Tell me who did it." The chill in his tone causes my skin to prickle.

I peel my gaze from his. "I don't know. It was dark. He was wearing a mask." As soon as the words come out of my mouth, I'm positive that I did the right thing. He will be able to handle the situation better if he doesn't know who my attacker is.

Instead of responding, he does what he does best. He retreats to his office.

The rest of the day is spent in silence, with Jared barely saying a word to me. Even though we are in the same house, even though he promised that we can make it through anything, he spends most of his time in his office. I don't blame him for being upset. He's only human.

When night falls, I eat a quick salad alone in the kitchen and go to bed. He doesn't come up for a while. I'm both relieved and terrified about that.

At midnight, he enters the room. He doesn't switch on the light. My body tenses when he lies down next to me.

He doesn't reach out to touch me, to comfort me. He falls asleep five minutes later. I don't. As usual, I stay awake for most of the night, terrified of what tomorrow will bring.

CHAPTER 15

I feel the touch of Jared's gaze on my face before I even open my blurry eyes. When I finally do, after steeling myself for whatever comes next, I have to blink several times to make sure I'm seeing right.

He's not only standing next to the bed on my side with a huge grin, he's carrying a breakfast tray. A thin stream of steam is rising from the cup upward.

I rub my eyes. This can't be right.

Yesterday, when he slipped into bed next to me, I felt the heat of his anger. Now this. He usually works off his anger behind the closed door of his office and comes out pretending nothing happened, but I expected this time to be different.

I tried to run away from our marriage. He knows I'm an escaped convict. I told him about the rape and the baby. I wouldn't have been surprised if he woke up ready to kick me out or send me to prison.

I search his face and find no trace of anger. I sit up in bed, unsure whether to be relieved or suspicious of his behavior. My gut warns me to stay on guard. This could be the calm before a huge storm.

"Good morning, my beautiful wife." His grin widens. "I brought you breakfast in bed." He lowers the tray onto my lap.

"Morning." I look at the food, then back up at him. "Jared, I think we should talk."

"About what?" He sits next to me on the bed. My skin prickles with anxiety when he touches my cheek. "Why do you look so tense?"

"Yesterday I told you that I was—"

"To hell with yesterday," he cuts in. "You're back home. That's all that matters to me. I took the day off so we can spend it together."

I can't help wondering if something is wrong with him. He's acting like someone with a split personality.

While I try to adjust to this version of him, he rises from the bed again and opens the wardrobe. He takes out a bright yellow dress, which he drapes over his arm.

"This is for you. I bought it a few days ago. We're not going out today because you need to rest, but I think you should put it on for me."

"I don't want to," I say softly. "I prefer jeans at home." I hate going back to being told what I should and shouldn't wear, being treated like a child.

"Don't be so ungrateful, my love." A dark shadow flits across his features and disappears almost immediately. "You will wear the dress and we will have a lovely day together." He hangs the dress on the back of a chair and walks over to me.

He picks up a strawberry and brings it to my lips. "You must eat."

My eyes remain on his face while my lips tremble open. My teeth sink into the soft flesh of the sweet fruit. It tastes so good, but I can't let him know that. I don't trust him. This could be a test. He could be waiting for me to relax before he brings out his other side.

I eat without showing any sort of emotion. He feeds me every bite, pushing my hands away when I try to hold the food myself. He even lifts the mug of tea to my lips.

When the food is eaten and the tea is gone, he tells me to take a shower and wear the yellow dress, which is a little tight around my middle. As he admires me, he pretends not to notice.

"Perfect." He hands me a brush. "Smooth out those tangles."

I clench my teeth and take the brush, almost yanking it from his hand. But I have to be careful how I act. One mistake and I could end up behind bars. I'm at his mercy and he knows it.

The day goes by in a blur with Jared fussing over me like a loving husband while I wait on tenterhooks for the other shoe to drop, and it does.

After eating a tuna pizza on the couch together, he quietly gets rid of the box and switches off the TV.

"You wanted to talk this morning. I wasn't ready. Now I am. What do you want to discuss?"

"Okay," I say, my body buzzing with dread. "I think we should talk about what happened to me...the baby."

The smile melts from his face and he shakes his head. "No. We can discuss that later." He plants his hands on his knees. His grip is so tight his knuckles turn white. "I need to know why you're on the run from the cops."

My body stiffens in shock. "What?"

"You heard me. What are you running from?"

I stare at him in astonishment. "You said you knew. You said—"

"I know what I said." He leans back and crosses his arms, his eyes fixed on the blank TV screen. "I don't know the details, but your Internet search history suggested that you're hiding something. In the last two weeks, you've been searching about how to be the perfect fugitive and looking up the best cities to hide. So tell me, Kelsey, are you a criminal?"

"You liar," I say between clenched teeth.

"You said you knew everything. You tricked me into coming back with you."

"What did you expect me to do?" His voice is too calm and controlled. "I did what had to be done to bring my wife home."

I shoot to my feet and grab my hair on both sides, turning in circles like a mad person. Driven by a burst of anger, I halt and face him head-on, my cheeks hot with fury. "Fine, if you want to know, I'll tell you. I'm done. I'm done pretending I'm someone I'm not." I sink back onto the couch. "When I was seventeen, I was wrongfully convicted of my grandmother's murder. They said I poisoned her. She was an evil woman, but I never killed her." I grit my teeth so hard my jaw aches. "I was in prison for ten years for a crime I did not commit. No one believed me."

"How did you get out of prison?" he asks, his face giving nothing away.

"I was involved in a fight. One of my cellmates attacked me badly. I had to be taken to the nearest hospital. On the way there, we had an accident. The guards died and I escaped." I shrug. "Go ahead, Jared. Call the cops on me."

As I wait for him to respond, his phone suddenly rings. His eyes still on me, he digs into his pocket and pulls it out. After a moment's hesitation, he gets to his feet and leaves the living room with the phone pressed to his ear.

I remain on the couch, shuddering with both

anger and fear, but in a weird way, I also feel a strange sense of relief. Now that one of my secrets is out, I'm almost free. When Jared returns, I'll tell him that it was Victor who raped me. After that, everything will be out in the open.

Nothing comes close to being as heavy as a lie. Jared can either choose to turn me in or he can protect me. Whatever it is, I'm strong enough to handle it.

I close my eyes and listen to the distant sounds of him. What if he calls the cops before returning to the living room?

It takes a while before he does, and when he enters the door, his expression tells me that something is terribly wrong.

Afraid to ask, I wait for him to sit down and tell me himself.

"It's Victor," he says finally.

"What about him?" All the muscles in my body clench tight.

"He's dead."

* * *

Ten minutes after Jared tells me about Victor's death, the doorbell rings.

"I'll go," he says and stands.

I stay behind, too shocked to move or even think.

Moments later, he returns to the living room, followed by Rachel, who comes to a halt as soon as she sees me.

I can see she's been crying a lot. Her eyes are barely visible thanks to the skin around them being so swollen.

"Hi, Rachel." I stand up to give her a hug. "I'm so sorry for your loss." The right thing for me to do is to offer her comfort, but it's awkward having her in my arms. After all, I'm carrying her husband's child, a child he could never give her.

"Thank you," she says with a watery smile and pulls away.

"You should sit down." Jared leads her to the couch and brings her a glass of water.

In this moment, he looks like the man I married, the man I fell in love with, so kind and gentle. The unpredictable, manipulative man I saw a couple of minutes ago is nowhere in sight.

No one speaks until Rachel has finished drinking. Since she takes small sips and there are long pauses in between them, the entire process takes fifteen minutes. After she's done, she stares at the empty glass in her hand for another five. She finally looks up.

"I hated him for leaving," she says. "I was so angry that I wished all kinds of terrible things to happen to him, but this..." Her voice trails off. "I didn't want him to die. I wouldn't wish that on anyone."

"I can't believe it. I didn't even know he was back in town." Jared rests a hand on her back. "Did the police give any details?"

Rachel pulls a crumpled tissue from the pocket of her skirt and blows her nose loudly. "A fisherman found him in the lake. The cops say it looks like he has been dead for some time. They want me to go and identify the body. I don't know – I don't know if I can do it alone."

"You don't have to," Jared says. "I'll go with you. He was my friend."

As I listen to their conversation, my mind is racing, thoughts scattering in all directions as I try to understand what happened.

I don't get a chance to find out more because not long after Jared offers to accompany Rachel, they leave the house.

As I watch the car disappear down the street, the words Jared whispered into my ear before walking out the door taunt me.

"If I find you gone," he said, "I'm calling the cops."

He doesn't have to worry about me leaving. I'm too drained to even move.

My mind is clouded as I return to the living room and sit with my hands between my knees, staring into space.

Victor was a terrible man and he probably got what he deserved, but something makes me uneasy about the whole thing. Rachel mentioned that he's been dead for a while before he was found. If it's true, how was he able to send me a text today?

CHAPTER 16

A week after Victor's body is found, he's given a hero's funeral.

As I stand next to Jared and Rachel underneath the shade of a sycamore tree, I'm finding it hard to breathe. Among the guests are a few cops who knew Victor. Their presence makes me nervous for obvious reasons.

The fact that Victor has been dead for days has been tormenting me every day as I tried to figure out how a dead man could contact me.

I tried getting more information out of Jared, but he has barely spoken to me since the day he received the news. On one hand, I'm relieved that his attention is no longer on me, at least for now, but on the other hand, I hate being in limbo.

He's such an unpredictable man, just because he hasn't called the cops on me doesn't mean he won't. Maybe his silence is also his way of punishing me.

He *does* speak to me, but only when he has to, especially during the preparations for Victor's funeral, which he decided to take on because Rachel was too devastated to make any decisions whatsoever. As Jared's wife, the chore of planning the funeral also fell on my shoulders.

I have gone through a lot of discomfort in my life, but being involved in the funeral arrangements of the man who destroyed my life was the hardest thing I've ever had to do.

I do my best to keep it together. I need to get through the funeral, then I'll figure everything out.

After Victor's body is lowered into the ground, everybody gathers around Rachel, offering her hugs and words of comfort. The woman who had already been so fragile when I met her is now nothing but a shadow of her former self. Her eyes have sunken a little too much into her skull and her blonde hair is hanging limp from underneath the black hat she's wearing.

As I watch her, I can't help wondering how she would react if she knew who her husband really was and what he did to me. Would she still grieve him as much as she is now?

I wait until most people have had their chance to offer her their condolences before approaching her. I open my arms to give her a hug. Holding her, I feel as uncomfortable as I did the night we found out about Victor.

"I'm so sorry, Rachel," I say when we part. I don't know how many times I have said the words to her in the past days.

"Thank you, Kelsey," she says, blinking away tears. "And thank you for helping with all the arrangements."

I wave a dismissive hand. "Don't worry about it. It was Jared who did most of the work." I pause. "If there's anything else I can do, let me know."

"No." She shakes her head, her greasy hair swinging from side to side. "I have to learn to stand on my own two feet."

Jared joins us and also hugs Rachel, whispering words of comfort into her ears.

"I can't believe he's not coming back," she says loud enough for me to hear.

"I know," he says, rubbing her back. "But we're here for you. Whatever you need."

"You're a good man, Jared." She glances at me. "A good man with a perfect wife."

I cringe inwardly and pretend I didn't hear her words.

After leaving the cemetery, some of Victor's closest friends come to our house for a short lunch. I'd offered to cook the food, but Jared insisted on having it catered.

As I sit in my living room, I feel like a stranger in my own home, and I can't shake the feeling that everyone is staring at my stomach. Can they see that I'm pregnant? What if Jared told his friends that he had a vasectomy done? If he did, they would know for sure that I'm carrying someone else's baby. They would think I cheated on him.

My stomach is still pretty small compared to many pregnant women over the two-month mark, but I still feel self-conscious, especially knowing that the baby I'm carrying is Victor's.

Once everyone is seated with canapés and drinks, stories of what a great man Victor was are shared. Unable to listen to them, I get up to find a quiet place to catch my breath.

I retreat to our bedroom and sit on the edge of the bed with my hands in my lap. The breeze coming from the window makes me shiver even though it's a warm day.

Victor is gone, but it doesn't feel over. I'm still aware of his poisonous presence around me. The worst thing is that he will always be with me. For the rest of my life, I will see him in the face of my child.

Sometimes I wonder whether I'm making the right decision choosing to keep his child, but a few searches online assured me that I'm not the first woman to raise a rapist's child. I read stories of women who learned to love their children as they would have done if they were conceived through a loving relationship. I haven't come to the place where I love my child yet, but I will try. I'll have to take it one day at a time.

I don't stay too long in the bedroom. I wouldn't want Jared to come looking for me. When my heartrate slows down, I smooth down the black maxi dress I'm wearing and return to the guests.

As soon as I enter the room, all eyes turn to me. The stares follow me as I cross the room to sit in the only empty chair by the window. Were they talking about me?

When Jared throws me a disapproving look, I realize that maybe it was disrespectful of me to leave the room when everybody was paying tribute to Victor. It must have been so easy to notice the empty chair.

To my relief, conversations start again until all the food is gone. I help Jared take the dishes to the kitchen.

The doorbell rings when I'm exiting the kitchen. I open the door to find Officer Smith standing on our doorstep in his full uniform.

Fear sweeps through me and I force myself to stay calm. "Good afternoon, officer," I say as casually as I can manage.

"Afternoon, Mrs. Bloom."

"Call me Kelsey." I force a smile. "Can I help you with something?"

"I came to extend my condolences to Victor Hanes's wife. I was told I'll find her here. May I come in?"

"Yes. Please come in." I open the door wider.

"Thank you." He follows me into the living room and just as everyone had stared at me when I entered the room earlier, they stare at him. But this time, there are questions in their eyes.

He ignores the stares and shakes Rachel's hand, muttering a few words to her before walking toward the chair I had occupied.

"Do you know anything, officer?" Linda asks before the man even has a chance to sit. "Do you know exactly what happened to Victor?"

He glances briefly at Rachel as though he's not sure whether she will be able to handle whatever he's about to say.

"What happened to my husband?" she asks. Her voice breaks down with each word.

"Are you sure you don't want to speak in private?" the officer asks.

"These people are my friends," Rachel says, glancing from one face to the other. "And they knew and loved Victor. They deserve to know."

The officer clears his throat. "There have been some new developments. As I'm sure most of you already know, Victor had been dead for days before he was found." He accepts a glass of lemonade from Jared. "It was revealed that he must've been killed before being put into the water."

There are several gasps. The room goes quiet

only for the silence to be shattered by Rachel's crying.

I remain in the doorway, reeling after what I heard.

"Who did it?" Connie asks. "Who killed him?"

"Unfortunately, we don't know that yet. But we will find out."

"Are you saying that Victor didn't drown?" an old man with a hunched back asks.

"That's how it looks at this point. His death is definitely being treated as suspicious."

"How do they know that he was murdered?" Jared asks. His face has gone pale.

"It was clear from the autopsy report that he was hit over the head with a hard object. At first, we thought he must have hit a rock in the lake, but there are obvious signs of foul play."

"Oh, my God." Rachel gets to her feet, clutching her stomach. "I'm going to be sick."

I jump into action right away, showing her to the bathroom, but a hammer is pounding inside my head, the pain blinding me.

I stay with Rachel in the bathroom until she's done throwing up, then I usher her back into the living room.

Everyone gathers around her again, comforting her. While she's sobbing, Jared speaks softly with the officer.

"This is horrible." Connie brings a hand to

her mouth as though she's also about to be sick. "Who would do such a thing? Who would kill poor Victor?"

"It's our job to find that out." The officer brings his lemonade to his lips and takes a huge gulp. "We will do everything it takes to find the person responsible."

"How long?" Rachel asks, her chest rising and falling rapidly. "How long had he been dead before he was found?"

"They think it's been several weeks already. It's highly possible that Victor never left town at all."

Later, after everyone leaves, I lie next to Jared, the weight of guilt pressing down on my chest. Like me, he's staring at the ceiling.

Two things torture me.

If Victor died several weeks ago and he never left town, there's a chance I might be responsible for his death. I struck him that night, but I can't remember how hard.

And if he died weeks ago, who has been stalking me this whole time? Who was pretending to be him?

CHAPTER 17

I lift my avocado, pear, and spinach smoothie to my lips.

The silence is unbearable.

Jared is sitting across from me, reading the local paper, avoiding my gaze.

I wait until he drops the paper to the table before reaching for it. I've been obsessed with following the news about Victor's death, terrified that the investigation will lead to me.

While Jared stares out the window, I scan the page dedicated to the murder, searching for clues. I find nothing new.

It's been five days since the funeral and the investigation is still ongoing. The local police have urged locals to come forward with any information that could help the investigation move along. According to the article, no one has come forward yet.

The autopsy results have finally revealed that it's likely that the day Victor disappeared was also the day he died.

I could be his killer. It was self-defense, but no one knows that. The mistake I made was never going to the cops after the rape.

It's too late now. If I go to the cops, they will throw me in jail, especially since I was already sent to prison for another murder.

I force my hand not to shake as I lower the newspaper to the table.

"I'm going to see Dr. Whitmore today at twelve," I say to Jared, my fingers crossed under the table. "She's my gynecologist."

I've made three appointments already, canceling the first two because I was not yet ready to face my reality. But I can't hide any longer. It's my duty as a mother to find out if the baby is healthy.

I'm uncomfortable telling Jared about my appointment, especially after almost two weeks of not talking about the pregnancy, but since he wants to know everything I'm up to, I have no choice.

I still have no idea where he stands. What hurts the most is that he never showed any compassion when I told him I was raped.

He picks up his cup of coffee and drinks it in silence. When he's done, he gets up from the table and walks to the door. Only then does he turn to face me, his face tight.

"Does that mean you want to give birth to a

rapist's child?"

As I struggle for something to say, he walks out of the room. Not long after, the front door slams shut and I breathe out. Every time he's not around, relief radiates through me. Alone in the house, I won't have to walk on eggshells.

I leave the kitchen and go to the living room window, where I watch his car peeling away from the driveway. Once it disappears into the distance, I drop into an armchair and grip the armrests so tight that one of my nails breaks. I don't care. I used to keep a perfect manicure because that's what Jared wanted. These days, he doesn't seem to care much. Aside from the day of the funeral when he gave me the dress I should wear, I now pick out my own outfits.

After sitting in the armchair for almost an hour, expecting every second for the police to ring the doorbell, I go on the search for the cleaning equipment. I'm glad I haven't thoroughly cleaned the house for a while. I need the therapy.

I spend a large part of the morning cleaning every corner, tossing the laundry into the washing machine, and making sure that everything is neat and tidy. Even though the house is pristine, my emotions are still in turmoil.

I'm not only afraid of the cops. I'm afraid of the person who pretended to be Victor, the person who had been stalking me for weeks.

Since that day in the motel, I haven't received another message, which makes me even more confused.

Am I still in danger?

With nothing else left to clean or tidy up, I jump into the shower and stand under the stream of cold water for longer than normal. As the water cascades over my body, I place both hands on my stomach. For the first time, I notice how much it's grown. It's real. There's a baby inside me.

I'm still terrified to give birth to a child when I'm too broken to be a mother, but there's no going back.

I squeeze coconut-scented shower gel into the palm of my hand and massage my belly with it, my eyes closed as I try to connect with a baby I did not plan on bringing into the world.

After the shower, I only have twenty minutes left before my appointment. I get dressed as fast as I can in a skirt with an elastic band and a wide T-shirt.

When I get into my car, the hairs on my neck rise. I sense that I'm being watched before I see Rachel standing at her window, staring straight at me. I don't know whether she sees me. When I wave, she doesn't wave back.

I arrive at Dr. Whitmore's office five minutes before my appointment to find several people in the waiting room.

The receptionist asks me why I came in. I whisper that I'm pregnant and came for my first checkup. I'm still uncomfortable about saying it out loud.

When I take a seat, someone taps me on the shoulder. It's Mary Jane, a woman who works at the Green Grocer's. She's at least six months pregnant. I don't know her well, but she's always been kind to me when I do my shopping. But when I greet her, warmth floods my cheeks. I was hoping not to run into anybody I know.

"I didn't know you were pregnant," she says, closing a magazine she had been reading. "How exciting."

"I—it's just my yearly checkup." I don't know why I'm lying, but the words pour out before I can stop them. After lying for so long, I have become an expert.

"Are you sure about that?" She leans closer. "I thought I heard you tell the receptionist that you're here for your first pregnancy checkup. I must have heard wrong."

I hesitate before responding. Telling people I'm pregnant without Jared knowing I'm doing it makes me uneasy. I don't think he'll like it.

"Well, that's a shame." Mary Jane sweeps her thick bangs from her eyes. "Wouldn't it be wonderful if the doctor discovers you're actually pregnant? Many women are pregnant without even knowing it."

"That would be a surprise," I say and decide to change the subject. "How's your baby doing?"

"My little man is perfect." She strokes her belly proudly.

Perfect. The word makes me feel queasy.

"That's great," I say, ignoring the bile in my throat.

"I'm excited about giving birth to my first child, but we might have to move out of this town."

"Why?"

"I don't feel comfortable being here after Victor Hanes was murdered." She shakes her head. "I just don't feel safe here anymore. We don't even know who did it."

My throat tightens as I nod. "But the cops are working on it. I'm sure we'll know soon."

Hopefully it won't be me.

"I heard they have a suspect in custody."

My body stiffens. "Really? It wasn't in the paper."

"Maybe they're trying to keep it hush-hush so people don't panic."

"Do you know who it is?"

"I don't know if it's true, but I keep hearing that it's Jason Marone. You know him, right?"

"Not really." I did hear his name mentioned a couple of times around town. Apparently, he likes to keep to himself.

"Well, he has been threatening Victor for

years." Mary Jane rubs her hands together, excited to be the first to share with me such juicy gossip. "Apparently; it was Victor who was performing surgery on his wife when she died four years ago. Rumor has it that Victor was drunk that morning. It was a big thing. But Victor denied everything."

"Wow." I twist my wedding ring around my finger. "Do you really think he did it?"

"It would make a lot of sense. He openly threatened to kill him once when they bumped into each other at the store. I heard every word."

"Oh." I don't know what else to say.

"Anyway," Mary Jane says, "I'm sure we'll know soon enough if he's guilty."

Not long after Mary Jane tells me about Jason Marone, the doctor calls her in and I'm left wondering whether what she told me is true.

Could it be possible that Victor somehow ran into Jason sometime that night—after I left—and they had a run-in with each other that turned deadly?

I hate to see anyone go to prison, especially a man who is still hurting after the loss of his wife, but the thought of bringing my baby into the world behind prison bars scares me.

Even though I feel like a terrible person for thinking it, I would prefer for someone else to take the fall instead of me.

CHAPTER 18

Dr. Celine Whitmore is a small African-American woman with salt and pepper hair wrapped in a knot on top of her head.

Smiling brightly, she extends her hand and gives me a strong handshake. She's somewhere in her fifties, but her skin is smooth and unlined. I feel tired and old next to her. I probably aged a bit in the past few weeks.

The examination doesn't take long.

"You are definitely pregnant," she says when we leave the examination room and take a seat in her office.

"Are you sure?" I ask her for the fourth time, even though I do feel pregnant and saw the baby on the screen.

"Very sure." She laughs. Her fingers tap the keyboard of her computer, but she glances up with a smile. "You heard the heartbeat and it was nice and strong."

I blink the moisture from my eyes. Watching

the tiny baby on the screen and listening to the heartbeat has shifted something inside me.

I wasn't sure whether I would be able to love the child, but on screen it looked so small and fragile that I couldn't help feeling something. With the rush of warmth that flooded my veins, my motherly instinct also took me by surprise.

Now that it's real, it's clear what I have to do. I have to protect my child. No matter what happens between me and Jared, the baby will be my top priority. Even though it was delivered in the most unpleasant way, it's still a gift.

When my tears refuse to stop, Dr. Whitmore hands me a tissue. I wipe my eyes and blow my nose before wrapping my fingers tightly around the damp tissue.

"Tell me everything I need to do to make sure the baby is healthy."

Dr. Whitmore explains all the tests I still have to do in order to confirm that the baby is fine. "Most importantly, you need to take care of yourself. Eat and sleep well. Keep that blood pressure low. It was too high for my liking. We have to monitor it." She hands me the ultrasound photo and I hold it so tight it's in danger of being crumpled.

A knock on the door startles both of us.

Dr. Whitmore asks the person to enter.

The door opens and I let out a silent gasp.

"Jared? What are you doing here?" When I

told him about the appointment, I never expected him to come with me.

Instead of acknowledging me, he moves across the room and shakes the doctor's hand. "Good afternoon, Dr. Whitmore. I'm Jared Bloom, Kelsey's husband."

"Very nice to meet you, Mr. Bloom. We were just wrapping up. It's a shame you were not able to see the baby live."

Jared doesn't even react. His face is hard as stone and his eyes don't meet mine. "That's fine. I actually came because I wanted to ask you a question." He pushes his hands into his pockets. "Is it too late to get rid of the baby?"

Both his tone and his words send chills down my spine.

A flicker of confusion crosses the doctor's face. Her gaze moves from Jared to me and back again. "Well," she says in a low voice. "Up to twenty-four weeks should be fine, but I thought—"

"You thought right, doctor," I snap. "Please forget what my husband said. I'm keeping my baby." With that, I storm out of the room, followed by Jared.

Outside on the pavement, my eyes are hot with rage and my hands are clenched into fists at my sides as I turn on him.

"How dare you!" I don't bother to lower my voice. I don't care that the people passing by are staring. I don't care what anybody thinks right now. "How dare you ask the doctor that question? For your information, I'm keeping the baby." I swallow the sob rising in my throat and glare at him. "If you don't want to be a part of this, you don't have to be. I wanted to leave. You're the one who brought me back." I attempt to walk away, but he shoots out a hand to grab my arm.

"Don't you dare walk away from me." He tightens his grip on my forearm. "I brought you back because you are my wife. We made vows to each other and I take mine seriously." His tone is dangerously low. "Now we need to solve this mess before we can move on with our lives."

"This mess is mine," I retort. "I'll handle it my way. Now let go of me." I yank my arm from him. "Don't ever touch me like that again."

My newfound courage takes me by surprise. I'm stepping on dangerous ground, but I can't hold back. The baby is giving me strength I never knew I had.

He follows me the short distance to my car. A few days after he brought me back home, he had someone drive it back from Polson. I don't know if he removed the tracker, but I don't care. I don't plan on going anywhere soon. Not when I'm pregnant.

When I get into the car, I lock the doors so he can't get in. He curses under his breath and pushes his hands through the passenger window—which is open a crack—grabbing the window pane.

"You know I never wanted a child," he growls, bringing his face close to the window. "So, don't be surprised by my reaction. How do you think it feels to know that my wife is pregnant with another man's child, a stranger's child?"

"How do you think it feels to be raped and find out you're pregnant with the baby of the man that hurt you?" I'm shouting now. "This baby was not planned, but I'm keeping it. It's my child, too. If you expect me to get rid of it, you can go to hell."

"Be careful how you speak to me, Kelsey." His withering glare makes me stiffen in my seat. "Don't forget that I'm the one keeping you out of prison." His mouth takes on an unpleasant twist. "Besides, how do I even know you're telling the truth?"

"What are you trying to say?" I throw him a scathing look. "What exactly are you implying, Jared?"

"Maybe you had an affair. How would I know?"

"How could you say something like that? I have never..." My throat thickens so much with tears that I can't get any more words out. I close my eyes, take a breath, and try again. "I'm not doing this right now. See you at home." Without another glance at him, I start the car and allow it to move forward.

"What the hell do you think you're doing?" he shouts, but steps back before the car drags him along the street.

As I drive away from him, careful not to speed, the sound of his angry voice cuts through the air. I don't care what he's saying. I need to get away from him for a while.

The thought of escape sneaks into my mind again, but I've learned the hard way that Jared will not let me get away easily. He'll do everything to find me again. He says he wants me in his life because he loves me. I no longer believe it. It's an obsession and nothing more.

Not for the first time, I wonder if it was him sending me all those notes, pretending to be Victor. As I turn the thought over and over in my mind, it hits me that Victor never wrote his name on the notes, which means they could have come from anyone.

But I still don't get why Jared would want me to return to him if he wanted me gone. Could it be one of his mind games?

Also, what about the text messages? They came from Victor's number.

I release a frustrated groan. What the hell is happening here?

I drive through town for half an hour, trying

to figure everything out until I hit a dead end. I only stop the car when I come across a maternity dress boutique tucked between a toy store and a jewelry store.

I don't plan on buying any clothes, but looking around might be a welcome distraction. Right now, the thought of spending Jared's money while our marriage—if I can even call it that—is in tatters makes me uncomfortable.

The only thing I need from him is a roof over my head, food, and medical insurance, something I won't have if I leave him. If it weren't for the baby, I'd risk leaving him again.

As soon as I enter the store, I grab a cherry red maxi dress from a rack and take it with me to a changing room. I pull the door closed and sit down on the little bench, gazing at myself in the mirror. Blank, broken eyes stare back at me.

I force myself to breathe for the baby.

Minutes later, someone coughs outside my cubicle. I try to get up, but my knees are too weak to hold me up. I sink back down.

"It will be all right," I whisper to myself, my hand on my upset stomach. "We will get through this."

"Ma'am, are you all right in there? Do you need assistance?"

My head snaps up to see red peep-toe shoes peeking out from underneath the door gap.

I clear my throat and push back my shoulders.

"No. Thank you. I'm fine. Just...just trying on some clothes."

The red shoes move away from the changing room and my shoulders sink with relief.

After several more breaths, I reach the point where I'm strong enough to get to my feet, to face the world, to fight.

I leave the store without buying anything and hurry to my car.

I come to a screeching halt when I find Jared sitting in the driver's seat. He has a spare key.

"Get in," he barks. "And don't you ever pull a stunt like that again."

The thunderous look on his face warns me if I disobey, there will be a high price to pay. So, I do as I'm told.

CHAPTER 19

The local radio station is playing soft jazz music that's as soothing as the rose-scented bath water surrounding me.

I dip my hand into the water. It comes out covered in white foam. The soft evening breeze coming through the window makes it look alive as it sways from side to side.

I lean my head back and stare at the iron bars on the window, identical to the ones in the bedroom. Even though they still make me feel claustrophobic since they remind me of prison, I prefer to have them up. My stalker is still out there.

Sometimes I think it was Jared stalking me, but some pieces in the puzzle don't fit right. He has revealed himself to be a completely different man from the one I married, but something tells me it's not him.

I close my eyes and inhale. That's all I need to do tonight, keep breathing. I have been so tense the past four days. Seeing another side to Jared totally threw me.

Every time I look at him now, anxiety builds inside my chest, making me breathless. I'm finding it increasingly harder to breathe around him.

To outsiders, things would seem fine. Jared still pretends to be the perfect husband. When people are watching, he opens doors for me, kisses me, and holds my hand, even when I try to discreetly pull it away. He's an expert at fooling everyone.

Behind closed doors, he ignores me most of the time. It's a weird marriage that we are in. He still insists we sleep in the same bed and share our meals together like a family, but he barely speaks and never touches me. I'm pregnant and he doesn't even ask how I'm doing.

The day I found him inside my car at the maternity boutique, he brought me home and locked himself in his office until dinner. When he emerged, he told me he was hungry and in the mood for Indian food. He ordered the food and we ate it in front of the TV with neither of us saying a word.

I still can't decide whether he still wants me in our marriage. Maybe he derives some twisted pleasure from having control over me.

He has started choosing my clothes again when we go out. He has bought me several dresses that are clearly meant to hide the pregnancy.

As long as he doesn't harm me or my baby, I will put up with his weird behavior until the baby is born. I'm better off with him than out there alone with no money and no job. Right now, I'll take what I can get from him. After the baby is born, I will have to make some difficult decisions. I'm pretty sure that the baby crying every day is going to drive Jared insane, especially since he doesn't want any children of his own.

I sink deeper into the foam until it tickles me under my chin. The tension and aches melt from my body as the music washes over me.

The music soon dies and the eight o'clock news starts.

My ears perk up when Victor Hanes's name is mentioned.

"The town of Sanlow is still grieving the death of Victor Hanes, whose body was found in the Sanlow Lake. Even though the police questioned a number of suspects, they did not make an arrest. Until today. We can confirm that this morning, a local resident of Sanlow was arrested for Victor Hanes's murder. The police have not given any further details at this point, but the residents of Sanlow can finally breathe easy knowing that the killer is behind bars."

I sit up in the bath so fast the warm water spills over the edge and splashes the tiles. I drag my wet, warm hand down my face, from my forehead to my chin to remove the foam. I'm sitting rigid, the blood pounding in my ears as I stare at the white wall.

An arrest has been made. Someone has been arrested for Victor's murder and it's not me.

Was it Jason Marone? Does it even matter who it is?

The most important thing is that the baby and I are safe. I won't be going back to prison.

But why doesn't it feel that way? Why do I still feel the weight pressing down on my chest? Why does my freedom still feel out of my reach?

It's Jared. He knows my secret. He doesn't speak about it, but the threat of him informing the cops that I'm a fugitive hangs over me like a toxic cloud. One word from him and I'm back behind bars.

I pull myself from the bath, careful not to slip. The water is suddenly too warm.

I grab a fluffy bathrobe from the hook behind the door and put it on, then I walk down the short hallway to our bedroom, leaving wet footprints on the floor behind me.

I stop in front of the door, my mouth dry. It's open. I didn't leave it that way.

Has Jared come home early? It wouldn't surprise me. There are times he shows up without me expecting him. It's his way of making sure I never get too comfortable or think of escaping.

Every nerve in my body is on alert and alarm bells are going off inside my head. Jared scares me sometimes, but not like this.

I take a step back as my skin prickles with fear. My sweaty hand grabs a vase from a nearby table. Holding my breath, I push the door open wider with my foot, expecting the intruder to jump out of their hiding place, to attack me.

When nothing happens, I take a few steps into the room, my vase raised above my head. There's no one.

I lower the vase onto the bed only to notice a piece of paper peeking out from underneath the pillow. Another note.

With shaking hands, I pull it out. As soon as I read the words, my fingers open again. It flatters back onto the comforter.

Did you miss me, Porcupine?

I was wrong. I was wrong about everything.

It wasn't Victor or even Jared who stalked me. It was a man much more dangerous than both of them put together. A man I never thought I would see or hear from again. A man I thought was firmly locked behind bars.

The only man who ever called me porcupine because of the stubborn streak I had back then is Garry Tyler. I fell in love with him, worked for him, and finally betrayed him. Now he's back to seek revenge.

I want to move, to run, but my feet won't budge. They feel so heavy. My entire body is frozen, but my mind is going crazy.

I swallow through my parched throat, my gaze sweeping the room once more, searching for him.

I want to save myself, but most importantly I want to save the baby. It's thoughts of my baby that bring my body back to life.

Suddenly, I'm running through the house, checking every door and window, making sure everything is closed. Everything *is* closed except for the kitchen window, which is swinging lightly. It's big enough for a person to fit through and Jared has not installed bars on it.

I slam it shut and draw the sheer curtains closed. It might not be a good idea for me to run out right now. That's what he wants. He wants me to run straight into his arms.

It was stupid of me to think he would never escape from prison.

On trembling knees, I return to the bedroom, wishing I could call Jared, but I can't. I never told him about Garry.

* * *

I'm sitting on the bedroom floor, my arms around my knees. My body is cramped because I'm afraid to move a muscle.

My eyes are on the door as though I expect Garry to break it down and crash back into my life.

How could I not have suspected it could be him? I was so foolish to believe that that part of my life was over.

I cannot believe that after Garry I still managed to fall in love with another man who thinks he owns me.

I met Garry two months after I escaped from prison. He found me sleeping on a bench and rescued me. At least that's what I thought he did. He helped me change my name without even knowing what I was running from, gave me a job, and promised to protect me. I quickly fell in love with him. Everything changed when I found out how he earned his money. It scared the hell out of me.

It's a good hour until I get back to my feet and pull out my laptop, reminding myself to delete my history when I'm done.

At first, I misspell his name because my hands are shaking so much. Once I get it right, I hit search. Various articles pop up on the screen.

When I read the headline of the first one, dread rushes through me.

Convicted murderer and sex trafficker escapes from prison...

I scan through the first articles, which confirm my suspicions. Garry has been on the run for five months now. He could be anywhere, even in Sanlow, searching for the woman who blew his cover.

A few days before I escaped from his clutches, I threatened to call the cops on him. That was after I accidentally discovered a hidden room in his strip club, where he packed terrified foreign women like sardines and sold them as sex slaves.

Sickened by the sight, I confronted him. Big mistake. He threatened to kill me if I ever left him or breathed a word to anyone. That was the first time he laid a hand on me. It happened a few more times after that.

The last time he was abusive to me, we were outside on the pavement and someone saw us. That person was Rosemary.

My head is buzzing with pain as I delete the search history and shut down the computer.

I can't stay here and wait for Garry to kill me. I have to leave Sanlow and the only person who might be able to help me is the same person who brought me to Sanlow in the first place—Rosemary.

As much as I hate involving her in my life again, she's the only person I can trust right now, and she knows about Garry.

I decide to call her from a prepaid phone I had before I married Jared. I find it inside an old handbag in the wardrobe.

As soon as it has charged to two bars, I call Rosemary. She's surprised to hear I'm still in Sanlow.

"Why did you return?" she asks in her usual gentle voice.

"I didn't have a choice." I push a hand through my hair. "But I need to leave again, this time for good."

"Did something happen? Does it have to do with Victor Hanes? But I heard about his murder on the news. You should be safe now."

"I'm not." I pinch the bridge of my nose. "Victor was not my stalker. It's Garry. I found a note from him today."

"How is that possible? I thought he was locked away."

"Yeah, me too. But he escaped from prison. He's here in Sanlow." I press my palm against my damp forehead. "He's dangerous, Rosemary. I need to get away. I'm scared. I don't know who to turn to."

"You still haven't told your husband about your past life? Isn't that why you returned to him?"

"He knows some of it, but not about Garry." If Jared found out about Garry and my life with him, he'd have even more power over me. "He's not the man I married. Things have deteriorated between us."

Silence fills the line, then Rosemary clears her throat. "Okay, darling. I understand. When do you want to leave?"

"Tonight," I say without hesitation.

CHAPTER 20

As soon as I end the call with Rosemary, I stuff a few things into a backpack, including the money I still have from the first time I tried to run from Sanlow. It's weird that Jared never asked for it.

Rosemary said she'd send someone to pick me up at 11:00 p.m. Five minutes before the time, I grab my bag and head downstairs without switching on the lights. I'm familiar with the house enough to navigate it in the darkness. If Garry is watching the house from outside, I don't want him to see the lights on so late at night and suspect I'm up to something.

He can try to come after me, but I won't make it easy for him.

At the front door, I fumble for the key to let myself out. It's missing from the lock.

My breath solidifies inside my throat as I grab the handle and push down. It won't budge. The door is locked.

Left with no choice, I flick on the light and yank open the chest of drawers where we keep the spare keys. When I find nothing, fear hits me like icy water.

"This can't be happening," I murmur, frantically pushing my fingers deeper into the drawers in case I missed something.

Then someone coughs behind me and I whirl around so fast blood rushes to my head.

"Jared," I say, breathless. Beads of sweat push through the skin of my upper lip. "What are you…I thought you were at the fire station."

"As you can see, I'm not." His eyes are narrowed to glowing flints.

Confused, I glance at the door. "I didn't hear the car."

"That's because there was nothing to hear." His expression is a mask of stone. "I was in the house the entire time, in my office." He says the words slowly as though he's tasting them first before releasing them.

Earlier, when I checked to see if all the doors and windows were locked, the door to his office was locked. I didn't think much of it. He keeps it locked sometimes. But now the thought of him hiding inside there while I thought he was out of the house angers me.

"Why? Why would you pretend to be gone when you're not?" I hate that he's wasting my time.

"This is my house. I'm free to come and go as I please." His eyes flash for a second and he lowers his gaze to my hands. "Now tell me what you think you're doing."

My heart is a heavy rock inside my chest as I tighten my hand around the handle of my backpack. "I'm leaving, Jared. I'm leaving you and I'm leaving Sanlow. I don't belong here."

He nods, his gaze holding mine. "And you think it's as simple as packing a bag and walking out the door?"

I push back my shoulders and lift my chin in defiance. "Yes, Jared. It *is* as simple as that."

He throws back his head and starts laughing, his shoulders shaking as though an earthquake is exploding inside him.

As quickly as the laughter starts, it dies. Silence descends between us, long and suffocating.

In my mind, I return to when we fell in love and got married. I remember the promises we made to each other when we exchanged vows. I desperately miss the man I married. I wish I could reach out to him. I ache to pull him into my arms and kiss him for the last time.

But too much has happened. The rift between us is too huge to cross. Whatever had linked us before is damaged beyond repair by hurtful words, lies, and betrayal. I don't even recognize him. He's as much a stranger to me as I am to him.

He breaks the silence by tilting his head to the side and clearing his throat. "I thought I had made myself clear that you're not going anywhere. I own you, Kelsey."

"No, you don't," I say between clenched teeth. "I'm my own person. I don't belong to you or anyone else." I squeeze my eyes shut. When I open them again, I have made a decision. It's time to tell him the rest of my story. Maybe that would repel him once and for all. "Trust me, Jared, you don't want me here. I'm not the person you think I am. There's a lot you don't know about me."

"You mean to say you are more than a murderer?"

"I'm not—" My backpack drops to my feet and the force of his words sends me stumbling toward the nearest wall, my back pressed against it as my knees give way. I can't stop myself from sliding to the floor. I drop my head into my hands and tears collect into my palm.

He shifts, but he doesn't make a move to comfort me. I don't expect him to, but it still hurts so damn much.

When I look up again, his eyes are still cold. "What else are you still hiding from me?"

I wipe my eyes with the back of my hand. It's time. "In the past I did things I'm not proud of." I sniff. "When I met you, I thought I could start over. I thought I could leave the past behind and become a new person."

"Who are you?" he asks, his nostrils flared.

"A stripper. I was a stripper, all right?" The heat of shame rises up my neck. "When I escaped from prison, I had nothing and nowhere to go. Then I met someone...he gave me a job."

"As a hooker?"

"No," I say in a rush of words. "I never...I never slept with men. I danced for them." I pull myself to my feet, but my back remains pressed to the wall. Even though I was his girlfriend, Garry had constantly tried to get me to cross the line to the other side.

"In my eyes, there's no difference between a hooker and a stripper." Jared's jaw is tight, his fists clenching and unclenching as if he's desperate to punch something. "You should have told me everything from the start. You lied to me all through our marriage. I deserved to know that I was sleeping next to a convict and a hooker."

"I'm not a hooker," I shout. "And do you want to know why I never wanted you to know about my past? It's because you wanted me to be perfect. I gave you perfect. If I had told you that I was a stripper, you would have left me. I know how you feel about—"

"To hell with what I feel about hookers," he says between clenched teeth. "What matters right now is that you're both a liar and a hooker. You should have told me. You should have told me who you are a long time ago."

"That's not who I am anymore." I look up with tears trickling down my cheeks. "It's something I did because I had no other choice. You changed me. This life changed me. I wanted to spend the rest of my life with you. But we both know that's not going to happen. I need to get out of here. Now." I push myself back to my feet and attempt to pick up my backpack. He kicks it out of my reach before my fingers can connect with it.

"You're not going anywhere. You're not walking out on me after everything you did."

I toss my hands into the air and allow them to drop again. "I should have told you everything from the start. But I was afraid. I wanted to be the woman you thought I was. I did everything to prove I was that woman. I hosted the dinners. I baked the cookies. I did everything to try and fit in, to justify my being here because I never wanted to return to the person I used to be."

"You failed. You slept with another man and you're pregnant with his bastard." He glances at my belly. My hands instinctively cover it.

I part my lips to speak only for the beep of a car horn outside to break the fragile silence between us. We both stare at the door, then back at each other.

"Don't worry," he says, a satisfied expression on his face. "Whoever is waiting to take you away will soon get bored and leave. You're my wife. You're not leaving this house."

"You're sick." I jab a finger into his chest and he grabs me by the wrist. I yank my hand away, scorched by his touch. "Why are you even pretending to want me here?"

I thought he would leave me after I told him about being a stripper. I thought he would be disgusted and throw me out. I don't understand his obsession with wanting me to stay.

"Don't think you can just go out there and create a fake new life as if nothing happened. You are a murderer and if you ever walk out of that door, the cops will be all over you." He digs into his pocket for his phone. "I can call them right now if you like."

"I did...I didn't kill my grandmother." Tears threaten to spill again as my body sags from the weight pushing down on my shoulders. "She committed suicide."

"You're on the run from the law."

"Yes, I am, Jared, because I wasn't supposed to be in prison. I'm innocent."

"You went to prison because there must have been overwhelming evidence to prove you killed your own grandmother." He looks down at his phone. "In the eyes of the law, you're a murderer."

Hearing those damaging words from the man I thought I would spend the rest of my life with makes me sick to the point that bile rolls up my throat so suddenly I can't hold it back. I push past him with my hand covering my mouth and run to the guest bathroom.

After I'm done, I rinse the bitter and sour taste of vomit from my mouth.

I turn to find him standing in the doorway, hands in his pockets.

"I'm prepared to give you another chance. We can wipe the slate clean and keep you safe from whoever is after you, including the cops. But there's a condition." He lets out a harsh breath. "We can only start over if you get rid of that thing." He points straight at my stomach.

CHAPTER 21

"You've got to be kidding me." I glare at him in disbelief, the back of my throat bitter with the aftertaste of bile and fury.

How could I have been such a terrible judge of character? How could I have been so blind to marry a man who is capable of such cruelty? He played me like a fiddle, charming me in every way until I walked straight into his web.

He dips his head to the side. A smile ruffles his lips. "I'm serious. That baby you're carrying is the source of our problems. If we're going to start again, it has to go."

"I won't do it," I say, adrenaline shooting through my veins, giving me the energy to fight back. "It's my baby and I'm keeping it. I thought I made that clear." I have nothing left but my baby. I refuse to give up the only thing that gives me purpose.

"I'm not asking, Kelsey. You will do as I say." He sucks in air through his teeth and rubs the back of his neck in frustration. "Don't you understand? You were damaged and dirty when I married you. I made you. I gave you a life. Now look at you, you're dirty all over again. All my hard work has gone to hell."

"What the hell are you talking about?"

"Everything was going well for us. I made you into a perfect wife. Every time I looked at you, I couldn't believe that you had once been polluted." His expression contorts with disgust. "Turning a hooker into the perfect wife was meant to be my biggest achievement and I failed."

Blood drains from my face and I stumble back, my lower back meeting the edge of the sink. "You knew?" I whisper, but he hears every word. All this time I felt guilty for not telling him about myself and he knew?

"Of course, I did. Fooled you, didn't I?" He pauses to give the words a chance to sink into my tortured mind. "I've always known that you were once a hooker. What I didn't know was that you are also a criminal. It makes it so much more interesting, don't you think? You were my project from the start and I'm not someone who quits when things get hard. I intend to finish this project."

"Go to hell." I puff out my chest. "I'm not your project."

"Of course, you are, sweetheart." He takes a

step closer into the room.

"Don't you dare come near me." I'm shaking with both fear and the worst anger I have ever felt.

He stops in the middle of the room and shoves his hands into his pockets. "There's something fascinating about taking something that's damaged beyond repair and putting it back together to create something new." His eyes take on a faraway look as though he's looking far into the distance. "Nothing is quite as satisfying."

His eyes meet mine again. Undiluted evil swims in the beautiful sea of green. Not too long ago, I looked into the same eyes and felt loved and alive. Not anymore. His eyes now remind me of the dangers that lurk beneath dark waters. The man I used to love has an evil streak I failed to see when we met. Having his eyes on me now makes my skin crawl as if insects are all over me.

"I'm not your stupid project." I clench my fists. "And I want nothing to do with you ever again." I try to push past him, but he blocks my way with his arm.

"Not so fast. There's something else you don't know. There's a lot you don't know, actually. But let me tell you a secret."

I shrivel up inside. I can already sense that whatever he wants to tell me will hurt badly. The smirk on his face says everything I need to know.

"What I have to say has to do with another

one of your many secrets." He shoves me with his arm so I move back into the room. "Since we're being honest with each other, I guess it's fair to tell you that I know what you did."

"What—"

"It was you who killed Victor. The wrong man is behind bars for a crime you committed."

At first, I don't know what to say. The words form an invisible rope that wraps itself around my chest and squeezes, forcing air from my lungs. My body folds forward, my hands cupping my knees. I force myself to stand upright again, to meet his gaze.

"I don't know what you're talking about."

"Of course, you do, baby." He tries to touch me, but I smack his hand away. "If I were you, I would be more respectful. After all, I know all your secrets now."

"It was him." The words cause my bottom lip to tremble. "Victor raped me. I hit him. But I did not kill him."

"Are you sure about that?" Jared waits for a response that doesn't come.

What if it's true? What if that night I struck Victor so hard it killed him? But if I killed him, when we searched for him that night, why wasn't he at the place I left him? Could he have dragged himself away and died from his injuries later? Maybe he bled to death someplace else.

My hand goes to my mouth and squeezes it,

stretching the skin, my nails digging into my flesh. I don't know how it happens, but suddenly I'm on the floor again, my heart threatening to beat right out of my chest.

Jared kneels down in front of me. I flinch when he takes my chin in his hand and tips it upward until his gaze holds mine. "Do you understand now why I want you to get rid of that thing inside you? It hurts, Kelsey." He tightens his fingers around my chin. "You say you're no longer a prostitute and yet you flirted with my friend constantly. When he took what you were offering, you killed him."

"I didn't." It's hard to speak when my chin is aching. "I never flirted with him. *He* hit on me constantly."

"Don't insult me." He pushes my head back and his grip tightens even more. "I saw how you acted around him. How you laughed at his jokes, like that day in the kitchen when they came to dinner. I'm not blind, you know."

"Let me go," I say the words slowly, pulling away from him until he releases me. "I don't care what you say or what you think. That bastard raped me. I never did anything to encourage him."

"So you killed him."

"It was self-defense. I needed him to get off me. You were not there. You don't know what happened. You..." The words die on my tongue.

If he wasn't there, how does he know about it?

Jared stands up again and towers over me. "You're wrong. I do know. I have it on video. If I show it to the cops, you will go straight back to prison."

Everything is coming at me too fast. It makes my head spin.

Jared was there that night? But how is that possible? I found him at home. He has to be lying. He's probably trying to scare me. But the truth remains that he knows everything.

"No." I pull myself to my feet as well, but I'm finding it hard to stand. "Jason Marone was arrested for the murder. I'm innocent. I didn't...I don't think I hit Victor hard enough to kill him." The rock I hit him with was big enough to inflict damage, but I refuse to believe I killed someone. Maybe Jason Marone found him later and finished him off before dragging him into the river. I have to hold on to that. The thought of him being in prison for a murder he might not have committed makes my chest hurt. I know how it feels to be wrongfully convicted.

"You have two choices," Jared says. "You can either stay here where I can keep you safe, or you can go to prison. But if you decide to stay here, the baby has to go. It will be a constant reminder of what you did."

"You can't make me get rid of my baby, Jared.

What your friend did to me was disgusting, but the baby is innocent."

"I can make you do anything because you're mine. I own you. The sooner you realize that, the better."

"What will you do, Jared?" Even though my insides are shaking, my voice is surprisingly strong. "Will you shove pills down my throat by force to kill my baby?"

"If I have to." A vein is throbbing at the side of his jaw. "I can do whatever I want to you and there's absolutely nothing you can do about it. You are a piece of nothing."

Nothing.

The word slaps me hard across the face. It's a word that brings back terrible memories. It accompanied me all through my childhood. Not a day went by without my grandmother making me feel worthless. That's why I recognize the pain that digs deep into my heart and twists like a knife. That's why I forget that I'm afraid of Jared and lunge for him. My fists connect with his chest before he grips my wrists so tight I'm afraid they might break.

"I don't want to hurt you." He brings his face close to mine. "Don't make me do it." He shoves me away from him. I cry out when my back slams into the sink.

I'm doing it all wrong. I'm standing in front of a dangerous and unpredictable man. I cannot attack him physically. If he hurts me, he will hurt my baby.

I need a plan if I want to get away from him. But I still have one card left to play.

I stretch to my full height and face him head on. "You're not the most dangerous person I know," I say. "There's someone out there searching for me. He knows I live here. If you keep me here, I won't be the only person in danger. It's someone I dated and he's a very jealous man." I stop talking and dig into my jeans pocket, pulling out a crumpled note. "He left me this note. I found it inside our bedroom."

Jared doesn't bother taking the note from my hand. He just observes it for a few seconds before leaning back. His lips curl at the corners. "That was me, Porcupine. I left the note."

"No." The note falls from my hand. "No, you didn't—"

"Yeah, I'm sorry I forgot to mention it." He bends to pick up the piece of paper and tosses it into the bin. "It was a little game I was playing." He shrugs. "Sometimes when I get bored, I mess with people's heads. I heard you say porcupine a couple of times in your sleep. I was curious to know what it means. Now I do."

"You're a very sick man." I inject as much venom into my words as I can.

"I know." He chuckles. "And you're stuck with me." While I'm still reeling from everything that happened, what he has confessed to, he charges toward me and grabs me by the shoulders.

Without a word, he pushes me out of the bathroom and shoves me toward the stairs, yanking me back to my feet when I fall to the floor. Every step he drags me up the stairs, I fight and yell for him to stop, but he only laughs.

By the time he pushes me into our bedroom, I'm in pieces, too weak to do anything as he slams the door shut.

CHAPTER 22

I grab the door handle and pull hard. Like the one downstairs, it refuses to move. He has locked me inside. For the second time in my life, I'm being kept prisoner.

On the other side of the door, laughter explodes from him. It's heartbreaking to know that my pain brings my husband pleasure.

"Jared, this is not funny. Let me out." I ball my hands into fists and slam them against the door. My bones ache at the impact, but I don't stop. Maybe Rachel or another neighbor will hear me scream and come to my rescue. But do I want that?

My screams die inside my throat and I rub my hands to massage away the pain. I'm alone in this. Alone with a monster that calls itself my husband. If anyone comes to the house, it's Jared who will receive them at the door. If the cops show up, the night might end with handcuffs clicking around my wrists. I have no choice but to accept the agonizing truth that I'm stuck in Jared's web.

How the hell did I enter into this twisted reality?

A sob is stuck in my throat as I stumble back, my body shaking. I don't realize how fast I'm moving backward until my calves touch the edge of the bed.

I sink onto the soft mattress, running my gaze over the powder blue bed linen. It smells faintly of my favorite jasmine and ylang ylang fabric softener.

Even though the room is warm, my teeth are chattering. I jam my hands into my armpits, remembering the day my grandmother locked me out of the house. I was only eight years old. She didn't care that it was in the middle of winter and the air was bitter cold. She didn't care that I was only dressed in an old t-shirt and shorts. I had broken a plate and had to be punished. I was lucky to find shelter in the stables, where I turned to an old threadbare blanket for warmth. It barely kept me warm, but it was better than nothing.

Now I'm not cold physically, but the biting cold under my skin feels almost physical.

When I hear the sound of Jared's footsteps in the hallway, I'm tempted to rush back to the door, to beg him to open it. But then what? If he opens the door, I will come face to face with the monster in him.

The best thing for me to do is stay put so I can think. I have to keep my mind clear in order to be able to get away from him. I need to come up with a plan instead of reacting all the time.

But first, I reach into my jeans pocket for my phone. I need to call Rosemary, to explain why I didn't come out of the house to meet the man she had sent to rescue me. She must have called me several times to find out what happened, but I had put my phone on silent. I pray she won't give up on me. I need her now more than ever before. She's my only friend.

The pocket that had held my phone is empty. It must have fallen out while Jared was dragging me up the stairs.

Oh, my God. I can't even call anyone for help.

A cold shower of dread touches my spine. What if Jared found my phone? He would see the calls exchanged between me and Rosemary. He might even send her a text to say I changed my mind about running away. Rosemary would have no reason not to believe it.

I close my eyes and force my mind to think of another way out of my misery. Nothing comes to mind. I lift my lids again and my gaze lands on the windows. Now it's clear why the bars are up. Jared planned this whole thing from the start. He installed the bars not to keep us safe, but to keep me trapped inside the bedroom.

He knew the day would come when I would discover who he truly is and try to get away.

I lift myself off the bed and shuffle to the window, my head pounding.

From our window, I have a direct view of the house that now belongs to Rachel alone, instead of Rachel and Victor. The windows are closed and the curtains are drawn. She must be already in bed.

I walk back to the bed and lower myself into the dent I created in the mattress, my hands wedged between my knees. For a while, I stare into space, trying not to think of what Jared plans to do to me.

Forcing myself to be calm for the sake of the baby, I rise to my feet again and walk to the wardrobe. As soon as I throw open the doors, Jared's citrus and musk cologne wraps itself around me.

I pull his clothes from drawers and hangers, pushing my hands into pockets. I don't know what I'm searching for. Maybe I'm searching for clues that would help me better understand the way his twisted mind works. I find nothing.

There's nothing else in the room for me to search through. Aside from the bed, the wardrobe, and a small dresser, it's bare.

Jared has always insisted that he wanted the bedroom to be just for sleeping. No TV, no desk, nothing else but the necessities. He calls himself a minimalist, never wanting a room to be cluttered. But now the truth is out in the open. It was all building up to this moment. He knew this room would become my prison.

I lie down on the bed, too exhausted to do anything else. Curled up in a fetal position, I shut my eyes, listening for sounds outside the room. Since we live on a quiet street, there's not much to hear at night. I'm not even sure whether Jared is still in the house. I can no longer hear his movements.

Without planning to, I fall asleep and jolt awake at the sound of his footfalls on the stairs followed by a soft whistle.

Disoriented, I sit up and wait for him to open the door. He doesn't. Not immediately. Instead, he remains outside, whistling louder now, torturing me. When he finally speaks, I shiver with both anticipation and dread.

"I will open the door now," he says. "I want you to promise that you will not do anything stupid."

I lick my dry lips and slide off the bed. Desperate to be let out, I hurry to the door. "I won't."

He probably doesn't believe me because at least five more minutes go by and the door is still locked. He speaks again, "I hope you know by now that if you betray me in any way, there will be consequences."

I nod as though he can see me from the other side.

"Did you hear what I said?" His voice is like thunder hitting my eardrums.

"I hear you." Hopefully he can hear me. I'm not able to raise my voice above a whisper.

The door opens and I back away, afraid to get hurt.

He closes the door behind him and leans against it. His eyes are softer now, but he won't fool me again into believing he's a good person. He's rotten to the core.

"Jared, please let me go. You never have to see me again." I bring my hands together, begging him. Fighting him gets me nowhere. I only get hurt in the process. "Please."

"I'm afraid I can't do that. I won't let my hard work go to waste. You're staying right here inside our home, in our marriage." He blows out a breath. "While you were up here, I did some thinking."

I don't say anything so he continues. "If you behave yourself, I'll let you keep the baby. But no one can ever know that it's not my kid. Is that clear?"

I nod even though there's no way in hell I'll let him raise my baby. But it's good that for now my child is safe. I have to play along until I find a solution. "Thank you."

"Good. I'm glad we're on the same page." He

rubs his hands together and a smile creeps up on his face. "Now this is what's going to happen. We're going to host a dinner again, like we used to do before you slept with my best friend. During the dinner, we will announce our good news."

"Okay." I press my lips together, doing my best to keep from lashing out at him. "What else do you want me to do? Anything."

"Do what you've always done. Cook, clean, smile. You're a great actress, just like I'm a great actor. This house is our film set and we are going to fool everyone into believing we're a happy couple. They will continue to envy us for our happiness." He crosses his arms across his chest. "I never wanted a child because I don't want some brat taking over my life. Now I don't think I have a choice. But as soon as the kid is old enough, it's going to boarding school. Are we on the same page?"

"Yes," I answer. I'll say whatever he wants to hear. But I'm determined to find a way out of this house before my child is even born. As soon as he lets me out of the bedroom, I will start looking for ways to escape.

"Perfect." A grin widens his lips. "I'll be sure to let everyone know about the dinner." He yawns, stretching his arms above his head. "It's been a long night. We should go to bed now. Tomorrow, we can start living our married life again from scratch. I have to say, it's a relief that I no longer have to pretend to you that I'm someone I'm not."

"Where do you want me to sleep?" I ask, my temples throbbing with rage.

"What kind of question is that?" His brow knits together. "We are a happily married couple, remember? You will continue to sleep in our bed. But I will no longer touch you in a way a husband touches his wife. That part of our lives is over."

Relief washes over me. I never want him to touch me again.

When I move toward the bed, he calls my name. "There's one other thing."

I turn around slowly, holding my breath. I don't say anything as our eyes meet from across the room. Seconds pass while I wait for him to hit me with another blow.

"You'll no longer leave this house without me by your side. We will be doing everything together, including the shopping. When I'm not home, you'll stay inside this room until I return."

My desire to lash out burns inside my belly like hot lava, but I keep it in check. I bite down on my lip and turn away from him again. When I reach the bed, my stomach grumbles. The sound reaches his ears and he chuckles.

"Someone's hungry," he says. "I'll get you something to eat. I'll be right back."

He locks me inside the room again when he fetches the food. I'm too hungry to care at this point.

He comes back with a slice of plain bread and a glass of water.

"Eat it or starve," he says pointing to the bread. "From now on, you will live on bread and water. The only time you'll eat anything else is when we have guests over." He lowers the plate onto the bed. "Consider it your punishment for trying to leave me. Next time, it will be something much worse."

CHAPTER 23

Jared and I are sitting at the dining table surrounded by his friends. They have always been his friends, not mine.

There are a total of seven guests at the table, three couples, and Rachel. The kids are in another room, being looked after by Linda and Don's nanny.

Everything looks the same, but it all feels different, damaged.

Unlike me, Jared is completely relaxed in his chair, smiling as he tells them a joke.

They all laugh and he throws me a look. A silent message. He expects me to join in the laughter. I do. I have to. I'm not yet strong enough to deal with the consequences.

Two days ago, I refused to sleep in the bed next to him. As a result, he denied me food for an entire day. The one thought on my mind that night was that by disobeying him, I was hurting my baby.

From time to time, he reaches out and touches my hand, squeezing it. The urge to distance myself from his touch grows stronger. But I'm not stupid. This is a game and I'm afraid to lose.

You are a great actress, Kelsey. You can get through this.

Today, I kept the promise I made to Jared a week ago. Like a dutiful wife, I cooked a tasty meal that made my own mouth water, but I was not allowed to even taste it while cooking. It was Jared who made sure the fig and grape sauce that was to go with the pork chops was the perfect blend of sweet and sour. I had to wait for the guests to arrive before I could eat.

Only a few minutes after I brought the food to the table, I finished mine. I was the first to clear my plate. The entire time I ate, I felt Jared's gaze on me. I never looked up.

The grapefruit tartlets I served for dessert also disappeared from my plate as fast as the pork chops did.

While everyone else digs into their dessert, I take a sip of water and stare at Rachel over the rim of my glass.

She lifts one of her three tartlets to her lips, but keeps lowering it onto the plate again without taking a bite.

She's here and not here at the same time. I guess she's finding it hard to celebrate when she's going through hell. I had been surprised when Jared invited her. In her place, I would not have wanted to come.

"Kelsey," Linda says, "you're so quiet tonight. You've barely said a word since you served us the delicious food." She presses an ivory napkin to her lips. "I always look forward to coming over. I can never get enough of your food. I was worried that you'd never do it again. Since Victor can no longer join us, I thought—it's awful what—"

"Honey, don't." Don touches her arm to stop her from continuing. Everyone's attention instantly goes to Rachel, who doesn't look up from her plate, her shoulders hunched, her greasy hair hanging over her face almost touching her food.

"I'm sorry, Rachel." Don throws his wife a look of disapproval. "It's terrible what happened to Victor. We all miss him greatly. If there's anything we can do, let us know."

"It's shocking that Jason Marone has been released," Connie cuts in.

"What?" The word leaves my lips before I can stop it. Jared narrows his eyes at me and I purse my lips to keep myself from saying another word.

"Yeah." Jared reaches for his water and takes a gulp that makes his Adam's apple bob. "I forgot to tell you, honey. They found new evidence that revealed that Jason couldn't have been at the crime scene that night. His alibi came forward."

"To think that the murderer is still out there is scary." Connie sighs.

As my pulse starts to race, Rachel pushes back her chair and gets up. "I should go. Thanks...thanks for inviting me."

"Oh, no." Linda covers her mouth with her hands, cheeks red. "Please don't go, sweetie. I shouldn't have brought it up."

"It's fine." Rachel gives us a watery smile. "I shouldn't have come."

Everyone takes turns trying to talk her out of leaving, but she shakes her head and walks out. Jared escorts her to the door.

"I feel awful," Linda says, a hand on her ample chest, fingers splayed.

"You should," Don scolds. "I told you to stay off the topic."

"Let's just...let's speak about other things," I say as Jared walks back into the room.

"I think that's a good idea." Pretending to be a loving husband, he kisses the top of my head before taking his seat. Then he reaches for my hand and holds it too tight.

"I don't know if this is the right time, but Kelsey and I want to share some news with you." His face splits into a grin.

"Really?" Connie claps her hands together.

"Good news, I hope."

"Very good news." Jared squeezes me tighter. "We are expecting a baby."

"Is that so?" Don frowns at Jared. "I thought the two of you never wanted kids."

"That's what we thought. But we're ready now. I never thought I'd say this, but I look forward to being a dad."

"That's…well, that's fantastic news. Congratulations to you both." Don raises his glass in a toast as the candlelight reflects on his glasses. His eyes are still on Jared's face. "After the last couple of weeks, we could all use some good news."

"You must be so excited, Kelsey," Linda says, a smile tugging at her lips. "How far along are you?" She tries to take a peek at my stomach but it's hidden by the table.

"Only a couple of weeks." I clasp my hands in my lap as heat floods my cheeks. It's a good thing Rachel left before the announcement. It would have been too hard to face her. Even if she doesn't know it's Victor's baby, I do.

"No wonder you didn't touch the wine." Linda winks at me. "Actually, Mary Jane from Green Grocer's mentioned she saw you at the gynecologist the other day. She suspected you might be pregnant. But I brushed it off as a rumor. I knew you and Jared never wanted kids." She gives me a once-over. "I thought you put on a little weight. I'm not saying that's a bad thing, but—"

"Linda, that's enough," Don warns to stop his wife from running her mouth again. I'm glad he does because I'm fighting the urge to slap her.

I give them all a tight smile and say nothing.

After all the congratulations and everyone patting Jared on the back, Don glances at his watch. "I think it's time to get the kids home. It's getting late."

"Yeah," Connie says. "We should also get going." She gets to her feet and reaches for Lewis's hand. "Let's go, honey." When her husband stands, she looks at me. "Kelsey, the meal was amazing as usual. We look forward to the next one."

As I say goodbye to the guests, my stomach twists with nerves. Their departure means that my night is about to get much darker.

When everyone has left, Jared closes the door and drops the key into his pocket. I no longer have a key. He argues that since I'm no longer allowed to leave the house on my own, there's no need for me to have one. I hardly leave the house anyway.

He follows me to the kitchen as I clean up. He doesn't offer to help, just watches me in silence. I wish he weren't following me around all the time. I would have loved to eat the food Rachel left untouched on her plate.

Even though I've had a lot to eat, my stomach still feels empty. My chest aches as I empty the remains into the trashcan and rinse the plate. After all the plates are clean, Jared takes out the trash.

When we go to bed, I expect him to bring up the topic of Jason Marone's release from custody. He doesn't.

I can't stop thinking about it. With the only suspect released, the cops will be on the search for the next one. That person could be me.

I force myself to sleep, but anxiety, hunger, and Jared's snoring keep me awake until late into the night. I finally give up trying to sleep and slide out of bed.

I notice that Jared didn't close the bedroom door tonight. Unable to stop myself, I head to the door and leave the room, careful not to make a sound. Without pausing to think about what I'm doing, I head downstairs in the dark and enter the kitchen. The red light under the fridge leads me to it.

The faint aroma of meat and spices still hangs in the air.

My mouth is watering as I reach for the handle. My heart stutters when I tug and the door remains closed. He locked it.

Tears pricking my eyes, I lean forward to press my forehead against the cool door of the fridge. I'm about to step away when I sense the atmosphere in the room change.

Light floods the room and alarm bells go off inside my head.

I turn around and our eyes meet.

"I left the door open to test you," he says. "I thought I could trust you. I was wrong." He folds his arms across his chest. "I'm sure you understand that you will be punished for this. I hope you had enough to eat at dinner. The only thing you'll taste tomorrow is water."

CHAPTER 24

I lean against the pillows and pull in several deep breaths. They don't satisfy my lungs. The air in the room is stuffy and smells of stale breath and Jared's cologne.

The only piece of furniture left in the room now is the bed. Everything else is gone.

My eyes are fixed on the bars at the windows. It's dark on the other side of the glass.

The desire to be free again eats at my stomach lining like acid. This is exactly how I used to feel every day when I was in prison.

Even though I still haven't given up hope that someday I'll be free again, sometimes I have doubts. As determined as I am to get away from Jared, he's equally as determined to lock away my freedom.

Three weeks. That's how long I've been his prisoner now. Whether he's at home or out, I remain inside the bedroom. The only times he gives me permission to leave is to go to the bathroom, once in the morning and once at night. The rest of the time I have to use a red bucket he keeps with me in the room.

The morning after the last dinner we hosted, when he caught me trying to steal food, he took me for a short drive, said he wanted to show me something. When he pulled up in front of the police station, I panicked. He assured me that he did not plan on turning me in as long as I obeyed him.

He forced me to sit with him in the car on the other side of the road for an hour, snapping at me if I looked away from the gray building.

According to Jared, the cops are still on the hunt for the murderer. I don't want to believe I did it, but Jared showed me a short video from that night, a simple clip that showed me hit Victor with a rock and him falling to the ground. The next scene was of me running. That was it. Nothing on the video showed how it all started, how Victor had followed me, or how he had slammed my head into the ground and raped me when I was unconscious. It only showed the scene Jared is interested in.

I lay a hand on my growing stomach and swallow the lump inside my throat. The only thing that keeps me going is my baby. He or she prevents me from going insane, from losing hope, from being weak.

It's late at night and Jared has gone to work.

Before he locked me inside the room, he gave me my usual dinner of plain bread and a glass of water. I worry that my baby is not getting enough nutrients since I'm not eating a balanced diet, or even enough food to kill my hunger. I never get more than two thin slices of bread a day.

When I think of tomorrow, a flutter of anticipation erupts in my belly. There's a Flower Festival once a year in Sanlow, attended by almost all the locals and a few tourists. I had totally forgotten about it until Jared mentioned it when we woke up this morning.

At first, he said we couldn't go, but when he brought me my food, he mentioned that he had been nominated for the Outstanding Citizen Award, which is given to the person who had volunteered the most in the community over the past year.

"You're my wife. People will expect you to be there," he said, his evil eyes sparkling. "I will take you with me, but only if you promise to behave yourself."

I promise to behave and a few minutes later, he shows me what I'll be wearing, a flowing baby blue dress with cherry blossoms on the hem.

My main motivation for wanting to go to the festival is because I'll be surrounded by many opportunities to escape, to merge into the crowds and disappear.

It will be a dangerous game to play, but it

could be my only chance to get away. I will never be able to forgive myself if I don't try.

I spend the rest of the night making mental plans of escape until I'm too exhausted to keep my eyes open. Morning arrives fast and I wake up to find Jared sitting on the bed with my bread and water, which is always served in a yellow plastic cup.

Without a word to me, he rises from the bed and leaves the room. The door slams and the lock clicks.

The bread disappears fast and I take my time drinking the water.

I've just emptied the cup when the doorbell rings. My whole body goes tense with anticipation.

The bell rings two more times, then the sound dies. Not long after, I hear voices.

It's at least half an hour before Jared unlocks the door. "Get dressed," he orders. He brings my dress to the bed and a pair of cotton underwear. Then he folds his arms and watches me put on the clothes. My body itches to take a shower, but I'm only allowed to wash myself once a week.

"I'm warning you again," he says when I'm done. "Don't do anything I wouldn't do."

"I won't," I lie.

He glares at me for a long time before he speaks again. "Rachel is downstairs. We're giving her a lift to the festival. If you don't want her to know that you killed her husband, you better keep your mouth shut."

I nod. He doesn't have to worry about that. Rachel is the last person I'd want to confide in. Where would I even start?

"You *do* realize that I'm protecting you, right?" He rubs his beard. "I'm the one covering up your crimes. The cops have been sniffing around and I told them we were both home that night. If you tell anyone anything else, you're on your own. You'll have no alibi in me." He lowers his gaze to my belly. "I don't think you'll survive life behind bars again, not in your condition."

"What do you want me to tell everyone?" I ask cautiously, careful not to anger him.

"Greet them as you normally would. If they ask you why they haven't seen you in a while, tell them you're having a difficult pregnancy. Most of the time, just shut up and smile."

"Okay," I say and follow him out of the room. My heart hammers against my chest as we descend the stairs. I feel faint with each step. My lack of energy has everything to do with the fact that I'm not getting proper meals and exercise.

What if the time comes for me to escape and my body lets me down?

Rachel is wearing a black dress, one that reaches to her ankles and her hair hangs limp on her shoulders. She looks better than she did last time I saw her. The bags under her eyes are still there, but her eyes look more alive.

I greet her with a stiff hug and pull away quickly. As we walk to the car, I notice her glancing at me several times, but she says nothing. I don't fill the silence.

When Jared starts the car, I look back at the house, hoping it's the last time I'll see it.

* * *

To my delight, the town is packed with locals and tourists taking photos of the intricate flower arrangements displayed on dozens of stands.

After we exit the car, Rachel comes to my side and touches my arm.

"Is everything all right with you?" Her eyes are flickering with curiosity.

"Yes," I say, aware of Jared's eyes on me as he gets out of the car.

"Oh." She frowns. "Jared said you were not feeling well. Your pregnancy is tough, huh? It must be hard for a person who likes to be perfect."

My shoulders tense up. "What do you mean?"

She shrugs. "I'm sorry, I don't mean to offend you. It's just that before you got pregnant, everything in your life was perfect. Now you're too sick to host your perfect dinners, or to even leave the house." She hoists her handbag higher up on her shoulder. "I'm sorry you have to go through that."

Before I can respond, she walks away to speak

to someone she knows and Jared appears at my side.

"It's time to have some fun." He kisses me on the cheek and reaches for my hand, leading me into the sea of people.

CHAPTER 25

The music and the laughter is loud, the air fresh with the scent of blooms. Everyone is bubbling with happiness. Except me.

I'm desperate to get away, to detach myself from Jared, but he's by my side the entire time, holding my hand.

Each person we come across hears the same story. We are excited about the baby, but I've been feeling unwell and we don't plan on staying long. My throat aches with words I'm dying to say, but I bite my tongue.

As we push our way through the throng of people, Jared puts a tight arm around my waist, his fingers digging into the side of my belly.

"Hungry?" he asks when we walk past a food stand. I don't respond. I don't want to seem too desperate for food. He could be testing me.

To my surprise, he pulls out his wallet and buys me a meat pie, then he leads me to two empty chairs.

I'm grateful for something to eat. I need the energy to do what I have to do.

When my tongue comes into contact with the meaty sauce, I swoon inwardly. The food tastes so good I almost forget my plans of getting away. Eating something different from bread and water makes me feel like I'm in heaven.

As soon as the last crumb is gone, the music stops and a male voice booms through the speakers. It's Travis McCleary, the mayor of Sanlow, a boulder of a man with a bushy, gray beard. He's wearing a green suit that, even from a distance, looks too tight around the belly.

People lift their chairs and benches to get closer to the raised stage while still remaining under the shade of the trees that surround the town square.

The mayor reads out his speech, thanking everyone for coming to the event. His speech is identical to the one he gave last year. He must have kept it tucked away somewhere in his house.

When I arrived in Sanlow, almost two years ago, it was the day of the festival and I was one of the outsiders.

After a while, the mayor folds up the piece of paper and pushes it into an inside pocket of his jacket. He's silent for a moment. A deep sigh is heard over the speakers.

"Although today is a good day, it cannot be

great because someone is missing. Victor Hanes, one of our own, was brutally taken away from us. No words can express how much we all miss him."

While an invisible dagger twists in my gut, all around me tissues and handkerchiefs are pulled out of bags and pockets. Tears are wiped away. The only thing I can do is bow my head to hide the truth.

Next to me, Jared sniffs.

The mayor blows his nose loudly and continues. "It's a tragedy that has shaken our town to the core." He pauses to sigh again. "I'm grateful to everyone who did everything in their power to take care of Rachel, Victor's widow. I hope you continue to do so. Victor will forever be remembered in this town and the cops will do everything to find the person who is responsible."

When the whispers break out, I find it hard to breathe. I'm relieved when an old woman not too far from where I'm sitting suspects that the killer must be an outsider. I pray that by the time they figure out that I was with Victor that night, I'll be long gone.

Jared plants a hand on my shoulder and squeezes. I have no idea what he's trying to communicate to me. I keep my head bowed until the mayor changes the subject. He spends a while talking about all the beautiful flowers at the stands and the delicious food.

"Are you okay?" Jared asks, shifting his chair closer to mine. It takes all my strength not to move away.

"I'm fine," I mumble. "I'm just tired."

"Don't worry. As soon as I get the award, we'll leave. There's not much left to do here anyway except sniff flowers and dance. I don't think you're up to it, are you?"

"I...maybe," I blurt out. We can't leave too soon. I need time to figure out a way to escape. "It's been a while since I danced."

"Fine," he says and returns his attention to the stage. "We'll dance, but not for long."

Before I can say another word, the mayor brings up Victor's name again and the cold knot inside my stomach tightens.

"We had thought of canceling this year's festival, but Victor would not want that," he says. "He would want us to continue the tradition of honoring this town and its people. This year, we want to honor another one of our citizens, a man who has been very active in the community."

When I glance at Jared's face, my stomach rolls with disgust.

The people of Sanlow have a way of making their citizens feel special. How would they feel if they knew that they are honoring a monster? But if it turns out that I killed Victor, they would probably think I'm the monster.

"Jared Bloom, I'm talking about you." The mayor points a finger at Jared. He pulls a gold medal from his pocket. It dangles in the air for all to see. "Come on up here, young man."

When the clapping starts, Jared gets to his feet, a huge grin on his face. He hesitates before moving forward, gazing from me to the mayor.

"Come on, Jared, don't be so humble." The mayor laughs. He accepts what looks like a certificate from a man next to him. "Come and get your award. You don't have to bring your pregnant wife on the stage with you. Let her relax."

The tension on Jared's face tells me he has realized his mistake. He should have chosen seats much closer to the stage. He's right to worry that if he leaves me, I might walk away. My muscles are already tight with the need to run.

At first, I'm afraid he will ask me to go up anyway, but someone from the crowd pats him on the back and nudges him forward. The look he gives me before stepping forward is one that leaves me cold. He's still smiling, but even though he's able to fool everyone else, I see the evil in his eyes, the warning.

Can I run from him? Do I have a choice?

With each step he takes forward, he throws a glance over his shoulder.

I wait with bated breath until he gets up on the stage, still glancing my way. My luck comes when the mayor engulfs him in a hug. For a moment, Jared's face is turned away from me.

I don't waste time. I get to my feet and move away as fast as I can on shaky legs.

"Where are you going?" I stiffen when Rachel's voice comes out of nowhere. I consider stopping to speak to her, but since she was rude to me earlier, I figure she might understand why I don't.

I keep moving faster, my head bowed, my upper body folded so it would be hard for Jared to see me over the heads of the standing people. A quick glance over my shoulder tells me that Rachel is nowhere to be seen.

Over the speakers, I can still hear the mayor talking to Jared. It would be impolite of him to walk away.

Weaving my way through the many people is hard and I'm already weak with anxiety. My upper lip and my armpits are damp with sweat.

I need to keep going. I cannot stop.

I step over empty bottles, candy wrappers, and chips packets on the ground. A man curses when I bump into him, but there's no time to look back, to apologize.

I run.

When I finally break away from the crowd and come to the large parking lot near the stores closest to the square, I freak out. Where will I go now? Where can I hide? All the shops are closed because of the festival, and I don't have a car to drive out of town. If I decide to walk, it's only a matter of time before Jared finds me. He might even ask people to look for me. I'm pregnant and tired. There's no way I'd get far.

From where I stand, I can still hear the sounds of celebration. I'm still close to danger. He must be frantically searching for me now.

For a few minutes, I wander around the parked cars, grateful that they are giving me temporary cover.

An idea drops into my mind and my gaze drifts to one of the many tourist buses parked on the curb of the main street. I run toward them.

A very tall man, maybe a driver, is standing in front of one of the buses, smoking a cigarette. I can barely make out his face through the thick smoke swirling around his head.

I choose one of the two buses that are open and have no people inside.

I don't think twice before running inside the cool interior and straight to the back of the bus, where I crouch down so no one sees me, at least not immediately. On the seat close to where I'm hiding is a leather bag. It calls for me to open it, to search it for money or anything that could assist in my escape. It's hard to resist the temptation. I'm not a thief, but this is a desperate situation.

I unzip it and push my hand inside, but I don't

find any money or a phone I could use to call Rosemary.

* * *

The longer the wait gets, the more I tremble.

Maybe what I'm doing is not smart. Should I have kept running? No, I'm too exhausted for that.

It would be far safer for me to disappear this way. The only problem is that I don't know how long the tourists will stay at the festival. Or maybe it's not a bad thing if they stay long. If Jared is unable to find me among the people at the square, he might decide to search elsewhere.

I wait for what feels like thirty minutes. When nothing happens, panic grips me. Jared is a smart man. He could decide to look inside the buses. My only hope is that the drivers will keep him out. But what if every seat on the bus is occupied and the passengers immediately realize that I'm not one of them?

My mind begs me to get out, to find another place to hide, but my body refuses to move. What if Jared is waiting outside the door?

Rock music from the festival makes the air around me vibrate. Later, when I'm gone from Sanlow, I'll always remember the song playing. The soundtrack of my life.

Unsure what else to do, I shut my eyes and start to count. I stop at fifty-two because I hear a sound. Someone has entered the bus. He must be talking on the phone. I hear his voice, but no one replies.

It dawns on me that if someone finds me hiding, they will know I don't belong in the bus. Why would I hide if I'm one of them? They will alert the driver immediately.

My heartbeat is racing as I sit up. When I glance out the window, I spot Jared. Rachel is with him. She was probably watching me the entire time and now she's telling him where she saw me headed.

I crouch back down, my insides quivering.

The man inside the bus has finished his call, but not long after, more voices mingle in the air. People are entering the bus. I force myself to sit up again, to seem normal even though sweat is dripping down the middle of my face. I can no longer see Jared or Rachel outside.

A man in a jeans jacket peers at me suspiciously, but says nothing as he takes a seat in the second row from the front of the bus. I hold my breath when an old woman with a large mole on her chin makes her way to the back, toward me. As soon as our eyes meet, hers narrow.

"You're not from the Sunshine Home," she says sternly. "What are you doing in here?"

That's when my mistake hits me hard over the head. The people entering the bus are much older than me. They are probably from an old age home. No wonder the woman knows right away that I don't belong.

I clear my throat. "I just—" before I can think of something to say, she opens her lips to speak.

"We have an intruder," she shouts. "She could be a thief."

As soon as she says the words, people start rooting inside their bags and a younger man enters the bus and makes his way to the back. He might be the driver.

My hands are growing clammy by the second and sweat pushes through my upper lip.

"I'm afraid you will have to leave, ma'am," he says, running a hand over his buzz cut. "This bus is for the Sunshine Home members only."

Ashamed and terrified, I rise to my feet.

"She's harmless," a woman with a tiny bun on top of her head says out loud. "She's pregnant. Maybe she was tired and wanted to rest. It's crazy out there."

"Thank you," I mouth to her. She doesn't notice because she looks away too quickly.

"Very well," the driver says after a moment's hesitation. "But now you have to leave. If you don't, I will have to call the cops."

All of a sudden, the woman who had warned everyone about me starts screaming. "I can't find my pearls," she shouts. "I left them on my seat. She must have taken them."

"I didn't steal anything," I croak. "I don't

even have a purse." Before we left the house, Jared told me that there was no need for me to bring my handbag to the festival.

It's a good thing I didn't find anything to steal in the bag next to me.

The old woman doesn't listen. She continues to shout in anger. "Someone call the police."

To my horror, a cop walks into the bus. It's the same man who had questioned Jared and me about Victor's disappearance.

My throat closes up.

"Mrs. Bloom," he says in surprise. "What are you doing in here? This is a tourist bus."

"I'm sorry, I was tired. I needed to sit down." I lick my dry lower lip and raise my hands, palms facing him. "I'm sorry. I'll leave."

My hands are still in the air when I reach the front of the bus. But as soon as I step out, the first person I see is Jared, wearing the medal the mayor had given him.

There are several more people surrounding the bus. He must have figured out that there was something going on and came to have a look.

"It's all right, officer," he says. "My wife gets a little confused these days. It's the pregnancy. I'm so sorry." He reaches for my hand and holds on tight.

I want to pull away, to call for help, but he would be forced to tell the cop who I am and what I did.

On the way to the car, he pulls me to his side and whispers into my ear. "I warned you. I hope you're ready for the consequences."

CHAPTER 26

The short walk to the car feels long and painful with Jared's arm tight around me, his fingers pinching my skin.

People are staring at us. I see them through the blur in my eyes. I'll certainly be the talk of town for the next few days. But I can't find it in myself to care. It's only a matter of time before I leave this town behind. I failed today, but sooner or later Jared will make a mistake that will lead to my escape.

When I try to pull away, he pulls me closer. "Don't mess with me, Kelsey. It will only take a second for me to turn around and tell the cops what you did to Victor."

"You're a monster," I hiss. I want to fight him, to let everyone know that he's keeping me prisoner, but my punishment would be harsher than his. I probably killed a beloved member of the community, a man whose memory they honored not too long ago.

"It takes one to know one, sweetheart." He presses a kiss to my cheek that makes my stomach roll.

Finally, we arrive at the car and he forces me inside with only his toxic words. I hate that he doesn't even need to lift a finger in order to make me do what he wants.

His hands grab the wheel so tight his knuckles turn white. He pulls away from the parking spot carefully and drives me back to the house I had hoped to never see again.

The tightness in his jaw tells me he would prefer to drive faster, to ignore the speed limit, but he knows the cops will be watching. As soon as we're a good distance away from the festival, he hits the gas.

As the view outside my window becomes a blur, I grip the door handle with one hand and place the other on my belly. My stomach lurches when the car starts speeding toward the back of a blue pickup truck.

I guess I was wrong. He doesn't care about the cops. He thinks he's untouchable.

"What are you doing?" I scream when we get even closer. "Are you crazy?"

"No," he says without looking at me. "I'm furious, and I want to teach you a lesson you'll never forget."

I shut my eyes and grip the handle tighter. The tires scream when he brakes suddenly and my back presses deeper into my seat. My eyes fly open in time to see the other driver pull up at the curb. Jared picks up speed, ignoring the anger directed toward him with the shake of a fist.

When we reach the house, my stomach contracts with the urge to throw up, but I ignore it until it goes away.

"Don't do that again," I say, stumbling out of the car only to lean against it for support. My knees are still weak with fear.

"Don't tell me what to do." He slams the door and comes to my side. "Get in the house."

When I hesitate, he grabs my arm and pushes me toward the house. He doesn't have to worry about someone seeing him being rough on me. The street is quiet because people are at the festival.

As soon as we enter the house, he slams the door shut and locks it. The key goes back into his pocket. Before I can prepare myself for what comes next, he picks me up from the floor. If he had done this a couple of months ago, it would have been romantic. I would have been giggling instead of screaming at him to put me back down.

"You'll pay for what you did today," he says carrying me through the hallway that leads to the basement door.

Fear flushes through my body. When we reach the door and my mind registers what's about to happen, I struggle harder for him to let me go.

I don't do basements. I haven't stepped into one for years. When I was a kid, I slept in the basement. While some kids have their own rooms and a comfortable bed, I had the basement and a dingy mattress. My grandmother's house had four bedrooms, but she didn't think I deserved one of my own.

"You want to play this game the hard way?" He tightens his grip. Pain spreads through my entire body. I'm terrified it might reach my baby.

"Please," I beg. "Don't do this."

"You are making me do it, Kelsey. It's all your fault." He kicks the door open.

"No," I say as panic rushes through me. "I'm not going down there."

If he takes me to the basement, that's it. I'll be cut off from the world. People will come and go and not even know that I'm inside the house. I cannot go through that again.

My feet connect with the floor hard when Jared puts me down and flicks on the light. "Get inside."

"I don't want to. Please, I'll do whatever you want. But don't...don't make me go down there."

Jared pushes his hand into his pocket and pulls out his phone. "You have two choices. Either you go into the basement or I'll call the cops right now. Make a choice."

For a split second I wonder whether it's best to go to prison and get it over with, but the thought of experiencing the things I went through behind bars fills me with dread.

I walk through the door, my hands clenched tight, sweat trickling down my spine.

Before I descend the stairs, I look behind me at the man who calls himself my husband.

"What are you waiting for?" he growls. "Go on." He gets behind me so close his body nudges me forward, almost knocking me down the stairs.

I grab the railing and lower my foot onto the first dusty step.

When I reach the bottom of the stairs, I'm shaking, my armpits now drenched with sweat.

It's okay. You are an adult now. You will be fine down here.

If only I could get myself to believe it. I can't help feeling like a scared little girl again with Jared playing the role of my evil grandmother.

"Good," he says, his breath scalding the back of my neck. "This is where you'll stay from now on. You deserve to be punished for the way you humiliated me today." He grips the back of my neck and squeezes until I whimper. "If you betray me again, I will kill you."

Even though I don't want to believe he's a murderer, even though I want to tell myself he's lying, my gut tells me he means every word.

"No." The fear of death is enough to make me fight back. Without thinking about the consequences of my actions, I lunge for him, clawing at his cheek with my nails.

He hisses with pain, then he plants the palm of his hand on my chest and pushes me so hard I stumble back. My buttocks meet the dusty floor so hard pain shoots up my spine. I shouldn't have done that. He's so much stronger than I could ever be.

My hands go to my stomach. What am I doing? My baby has been subjected to so much suffering already. How much more will it be able to take? Is it even alive?

Before I can pull myself back to my feet, Jared stomps up the stairs and slams the door shut. The light goes off and I'm plunged into darkness.

I don't move from the spot. Inside my head, I'm back in my grandmother's house. Like I used to do back then, I draw my knees to my chest and wrap my arms around them, careful not to squeeze the baby too tight. I rock back and forth while gazing into the darkness.

"It's okay, baby," I whisper softly. "You don't have to be afraid. We will make it out of here." I don't believe a single word I'm saying.

I pull in breath after breath to calm myself, but it's not working. My body refuses to relax. How can I protect my baby if I cannot even protect myself?

After a while, my eyes adjust to the darkness and I force myself to look around. That's when I notice a tiny window at the far end of the room. It's so small and the glass is too dirty to allow enough sunlight to enter. I sit staring at it, unmoving, my body numb.

I'm not sure how long I wait for Jared to return, but it has to be a while because by the time the light is switched on and the door is unlocked, I'm hungry again, the pie I ate at the festival long forgotten.

He appears at the top of the stairs with a slice of bread in one hand and a plastic cup of water in the other.

"I hope you have made yourself at home down here," he says, smiling as he descends the stairs.

I don't answer and he doesn't say anything more. Instead of giving me the bread, he throws it onto the dirty floor and lowers the cup of water next to it. He leaves again, locking the door behind him.

My fingers search the floor for the bread. I'm too hungry to care that it's dirty. I find it and dust it off with my clothes as best I can. I eat it like someone who hasn't eaten anything in weeks. I don't get to drink the water. In my desperation to drink it, I knock it over by mistake while reaching for it.

That's when I quit holding on and cry, deep,

heart-wrenching sobs. I cry for the life I almost had. I cry for my unborn child. I cry because I'm so tired.

When there's nothing else left in me, I pick myself up off the floor. With the help of the faint light from the window, I shuffle toward one of the boxes. Even though the basement reminds me of the past, maybe it's the best place for me to be right now. Maybe I'll be able to find something to help me.

I have to do something or risk going insane. Maybe that's what he wants. He wants me to go crazy so he can have complete power over me.

Blocking out my childhood fears, I start searching through the boxes around me, looking for weapons I could use to defend myself.

Most of the boxes are filled with clothes, nothing that could inflict harm.

Just when I'm about to give up, I come across a photo frame. I snap it apart, separating it into four pieces of wood. They might come in handy.

Even though there are still many boxes I can search through, my aching body is screaming for me to rest. I lean against one of the boxes and close my eyes.

CHAPTER 27

When Jared returns to the basement, it's dark outside.

He doesn't come to me immediately. Instead, he stands at the top of the stairs, saying nothing.

I move my hands behind my back, my fingers curling around the four wooden sticks. How does he plan to torture me next?

I don't want him to come near me, but at the same time, the silence is killing me. It ends with the thud of his footfalls on the steps as he finally descends the stairs.

I make myself small, wedging my body between two boxes that I searched earlier.

When I look up, our eyes meet. A smile ruffles the corners of his lips and turns into a full-blown grin that makes his eyes crinkle at the sides.

He must have taken a shower not long ago because his hair is damp and he's wearing a clean white shirt and tan pants.

He pushes his hands into his pockets and rolls

his shoulders before meeting my eyes again.

"I'm disappointed," he says. "I actually thought I could pull this off without a hitch."

"Pull what off?" My voice is stronger than I feel.

"Maybe it's time to tell you a story." He picks up one of the boxes, placing it a distance away from me before sitting down on it. "I have a confession to make." He clears his throat. "This is not a real marriage. It was never meant to be one."

"What do you mean?" The last thing I want is to communicate with him, but my mouth refuses to shut up.

"It was all a game." He pauses for effect. "It started with one drunken night in Missoula. Two friends went out to have a good time and ended up buying a winning lottery ticket at a random casino. One of the two men had provided the money to buy the ticket, and the other bought it. That night, the two friends won $1.5 million." He stops talking again to give me a chance to take in the information, but my mind is clouded with confusion.

"To celebrate the win, those two friends headed to a bar not too far from the casino. The bar was attached to a strip club. More alcohol was consumed and when it came time to discuss how much each man would get, there was a dilemma. None of the two friends wanted to share the money equally. Remember when I said one of them paid for the ticket and the other bought it, right? Each felt he had the right to the entire fortune."

"What...what are you talking about?" Something is starting to gnaw at my insides.

"Don't worry, you will soon understand." He smiles wider. "To solve the problem, one of the men proposed they bet on something and the winner would take it all."

I blink several times, afraid to hear more, but wanting to know.

"The friends ended up in the strip club and one of them came up with a crazy idea. He pointed to a stripper and said that if he manages to make her his wife, and the marriage is still intact after two years, he should get all the money."

"Oh, my God." My hand trembles to my lips. "You...you—"

"That's right, my wife." He strokes his beard. "It was me. I promised my friend that I can turn you into the perfect wife and in two years' time, I would be $1.5 million richer. We both thought it was a crazy, but fantastic idea. My friend didn't think I could pull it off. There were rules, of course, and one of them was that you were not to sleep with any other man during the two years. If that happened, for whatever reason, the deal was off and the money would be paid out to my friend. The papers were drawn up by another good friend of ours who actually dines with us from time to time. He's a good lawyer."

"Don." It has to be him. He's the only lawyer we've ever invited to dinner.

"Bingo." Jared puffs out his chest. "The lawyer who drew up the papers was Don."

My stomach clenches and blood rushes to my head, making it spin. I'm too devastated to even speak.

"The reason I didn't tell you about my little game while I pretended to fall in love with you was because I was not allowed to. It was one of the rules of the game." He dips his head to one side. "I brought you to this town and made you mine. I was determined to fix you. At the end of the two years, I was going to discard you like an old dishcloth."

There are so many questions scrambling for space inside my head. He answers one of them before I can ask it.

"Since a lot of money was on the line, I needed help. Lucky for me, I knew a woman who was determined to do good, rescuing women from poverty and helping them start new lives."

"Not Rosemary." I shake my head, tears flooding my eyes. He has to be lying.

"Yep, that's her. It was pretty easy to get her help because she owes me. But that's none of your business. I told her to bring you to this town, give you a place to stay, and help you get a job."

My shoulders shake as sobs break me apart. I'm finding it hard to believe that the only person I trusted in this town betrayed me. She had stalked me and showed up in my life at the time I was desperate to get away from Garry.

She helped me escape in the middle of the night and urged me to make an anonymous call to the cops to report him. She told me about her shelter in a small town called Sanlow and promised to help me start over. She lied to me.

She couldn't have known about Jared's plans. Maybe he played her like he played me.

What does she owe him? Why would she go to such lengths to do his dirty work? Jared told me it's none of my business. But it is, and one day I will get the answers from her.

Another question slams into my mind.

"Who was the other man? Who made the bet with you?" If he's going to hurt me, he might as well dump everything on me so I can deal with it all at once.

"You already know." He pushes himself to his feet. "Come on, Kelsey, use your brain."

"Victor," I say.

"Smart girl." He claps his hands. "I made a deal with Victor and he tried to sabotage it."

"By sleeping with me."

"Yep," Jared says. "Too bad for him, no one

will ever know what happened between you two that night."

"You did it," I shout. "You killed him so you can get all the money."

"No, *you* killed him." He cracks a knuckle. "Unfortunately, his death does nothing for me. The money does not automatically come to me. I only get it if I'm still married to you after two years and there is no evidence that you slept with another man."

Eight months to go. Our two-year anniversary is in eight months.

Now I understand why he hasn't called the cops on me. Once I tell the cops that I hit Victor over the head because he raped me, Jared will lose the bet.

"Who will get the money now that Victor is dead?"

"Don," he says. "But we both know that won't happen. The money is mine."

"You are a terrible man." The words mix with the bitter bile on my tongue. "You're evil."

Jared shrugs. "That's what my ex-wife used to say about me. I'm used to it."

"You were married?" Surprise sweeps through me. How many more secrets is he hiding?

"I was, but it didn't last long. I didn't tell you because we don't have a real marriage. I don't owe you anything."

If he was married before, I'm not surprised it ended. She must have discovered his other side and bolted. Lucky woman.

"If it weren't for the money, I would never have married again. I'm not the marrying kind. I'm not the daddy kind either."

"What happened to her?" Now that he has opened the can of worms, I need to know everything. I'm hurting myself by digging for more information, but understanding who he is might help free me from his clutches.

"It was a tragic accident," he says, shaking his head. "We were on vacation in Hawaii and she drowned. It was even more sad because she was pregnant." He sighs. "I returned from the vacation a grieving husband. We lived in New York at the time. After she died, I couldn't stay. I needed to get away from the memories, to start a new life with a new name. My mother was born here so it felt like coming home."

"What did you do to her?" My words are so loud they scrape the inside of my throat. "What did you do to her, Jared?"

"You're a smart woman. Why don't you figure it out for yourself?"

He killed her. I'm sure of it. She got pregnant and he got rid of her. That's why he changed his name.

Jared is a murderer. The thought makes me feel suddenly cold. "Why didn't you just leave her?"

"That's enough." He slams a fist into his palm. "I don't want to talk about the past. What's done is done. Let's talk about you. I need you to get rid of that baby after all."

"Why do you want that?" My words are drenched in tears. "Why do you care whether my baby is alive or not? After the two years are over, you'll be getting rid of me anyway."

"Yes, but getting rid of your baby is part of your punishment."

CHAPTER 28

After throwing up for the third time in a corner of the basement, I wipe my mouth with the back of my hand.

The cramps raging in my stomach remind me of the emptiness inside me. I tell myself that's all it is...hunger and nothing else. The baby is fine.

Jared is serious about wanting my baby to die. That's why he's starving me.

I return to my usual spot between two boxes and sit staring at the small window. It's too high up for me to reach it and too small for me to squeeze through.

It must be hours since he left me. The view of the sky outside the window gives me an idea of what time of day it is. The sky had been black not too long ago. When the sun rays broke through the darkness, I knew it was another day.

I spent the night thinking about everything Jared told me. The secrets, the betrayal, and the look in his eyes when he confessed to making me a pawn in his game are all too much to deal with.

If I want to survive what's ahead, I have to take my mind off the torturous thoughts. Allowing them to eat me up from the inside will hurt more than just me.

I close my eyes, inhale the stale air, and force my mind to become as numb as my buttocks.

With no energy left in me to do anything else, most of my time is spent sitting. I only crawl from my spot to throw up or to urinate.

The basement is big, but it closes in on me with each breath.

As a kid, when I was alone in the basement, I used to pretend I had imaginary friends. They helped me push past the loneliness and fear. This time, I talk to my baby, a real person. I promise the baby that we will make it out of Jared's web alive, that I will protect him or her.

After fighting off dark thoughts for a while, sleep finally catches up with me. I want to stay awake, but I can't keep my eyelids from growing heavy. My eyes close on their own.

I dream that I'm walking in the middle of a highway, with cars whizzing by. There's blood and it's trickling down my inner thighs to my ankles. I'm not sure where it's coming from and no one is stopping to ask if I'm all right. I don't call for help. I keep walking until the strength melts from my body and I crumple to the ground, where I cry until I fall asleep.

When I wake up, I'm back in the basement. I'm not sure what the nightmare meant, but it doesn't matter. My real life is a nightmare. The bad dream was probably brought on by my deep-rooted fear of losing the baby.

I press a hand to my stomach and something unfurls to life deep inside my belly, gentle like the subtle touch of butterfly wings.

Tears of relief spring to my eyes. My baby is alive. It's hanging in there, refusing to let go.

"I won't let anything happen to you," I say, choking up. "I won't let him hurt you."

I'm making promises I'm not sure I can keep, but hope is all I have left. If the baby turns out to be a girl, I'll call her Hope or Faith.

When the baby stops fluttering, thoughts of Jared's words sneak back into my mind, how he hinted at murdering his first wife.

But what if it's not true? What if he made it all up to scare me? It would be much easier for him to control me if I'm terrified of him.

I kill the thought before it drives me insane with fear.

To distract myself, I crawl to the stairs, my long dress making it hard. With the help of the wooden railing, I pull myself up and tip my head back. Gazing up at the closed door, I climb the stairs one at a time.

After only a few steps, my body forces me to rest, every muscle inside my body quivering with exhaustion. I refuse to give up. I keep going until I reach the top.

I lean against the door to catch my breath. My lungs are hurting as if I have run a marathon.

I have no idea what I'm doing at the top of the stairs, how I think I'll be able to escape without a key. But I needed to do something.

"Hi, Kelsey," he says.

I jump back from the door, almost tripping down the stairs. I catch myself in time.

"I know you are there. I heard you come up." He chuckles. "Are you hungry? Would you like something to eat and drink?"

"Yes." I lick my parched lips and press my forehead against the door. "Please, Jared. Let me out. I'll do whatever you want. I'll be the perfect wife."

"I wish I could trust you." Chair legs scrape the floor on the other side. How long has he been sitting there?

I push my palms against the door. "You can. I promise. Please, open the door." Fresh tears spring to my eyes.

"You know I can't do that, Kelsey. You betrayed me once. If I let you out, you'll do it again. How can I be certain you won't share our little secret with someone else? I can't let you mess with my plans." He pauses. "You'll remain inside this house until our two years are up." The sound of papers ruffling pushes its way through the cracks. "But there's another way out of this."

"What? Tell me what I need to do."

"There's a clause in this contract that I totally forgot about. It says here that if you die while still married to me, I automatically get the money. I don't know how I could have missed it."

Blood drains from my face. "Don't do it. Don't kill me."

"No worries, I won't because this is fun. I'm enjoying this game. I love messing with people's minds. I did it all the time as a kid." A knuckle cracks. "There was a side of me that secretly enjoyed watching people suffer. I called him Jack. There's nothing Jack loves more than the smell of fear."

I don't know whether to be relieved or terrified at what he said. Wanting me to suffer could mean never letting me out of here alive, waiting for me to die a slow and painful death.

The day Jared brought me home from the motel, I wondered whether he had a split personality because one minute he was angry and the next he pretended nothing happened. He always deals with his anger behind the closed door of his office and emerges a different person from the one who went in. Now I'm starting to wonder whether he really does have multiple personalities.

"Kelsey, I'm sorry, but I have to go. I've been out here all night. I'll go and take a nap. I'll leave the tough decisions for later." The chair scrapes the floor again. The sound is followed by that of his footsteps as he walks away, leaving me with nothing but fear to feed on.

When will he return? How long will it be until he gives me something to eat and drink?

I'm much too weak to even return to the bottom of the stairs, so I lower myself to the floor and rest my head on my knees, trying not to be drowned by the darkness.

I remind myself of the first weeks in prison when I didn't think I would be able to survive. I was a seventeen-year-old charged as an adult for a murder I did not commit. I was locked up inside a cell infested with rats and cockroaches. I survived ten years in prison. I desperately want to believe that the strength I had back then is still somewhere inside of me.

I try to think of good times, positive memories. Everything that comes up is connected to Jared. My mind takes me back to the day we met and reminds me of the butterflies in my stomach. The day he kissed me for the first time, I thought I was the luckiest girl in the world. The day we exchanged vows was the happiest day of my life.

I made a big mistake.

I can't draw comfort from the memories we made because every single one of them is now damaged.

I drag myself back downstairs, afraid if Jared comes into the basement, he might decide to push me down the stairs just to see me suffer.

Even in my broken state, I won't make it easy for him to get what he wants.

CHAPTER 29

When the light floods the basement and the key turns in the lock, I don't move from where I'm lying on the floor. The little strength I had before is long gone.

I'm barely awake now, hanging on to consciousness.

The door swings open and I blink the drowsiness from my eyes so I can see better.

He fills the doorway and remains there, watching me with a smile. He doesn't get a reaction from me.

It's dark outside again. Another day has ended with me trapped in the house from hell with no one knowing what I'm going through.

He must have had plenty of time to think about whether or not to go ahead and kill me. I'm not even sure I care anymore. I'm desperate for anything that would make the pain go away, especially the emotional kind.

As usual, he doesn't come down right away.

Torturing me must be so much fun for him.

"Jared," I croak. "Please."

"Jared is not here. Jack has come out to play."

"Jack," I whisper. "Please...water." I'm so worried about the baby. I haven't felt it move in a while. I don't care what he calls himself as long as he helps me.

"Maybe I'll give you something to drink. I'm in a good mood." He steps back outside and comes back with a small plastic bottle of water and a loaf of bread. "I'll leave it here for you." He puts the food and drink on the floor of the landing. I'll be eating dirt again. I don't care. I only wish he would bring it down to me. But I know better than to make the request.

He brought me more food than I normally get, a loaf instead of a slice. Maybe he has decided to let me live.

"Thank you," I say. My mouth has already started to water. But how would I make it to the top of the stairs when I can barely move?

"One more thing," he says, his hand on the handle. "Give birth to your baby if that's what you want, but both of you will remain here until I get my money. I'll give myself time to decide what to do with you once this is all over." He glances at the food. "What's the matter? Won't you come and eat?"

I look up at him, pleading. "I—"

"Fine." He sighs and bends down to pick up

the food. "I'll bring it down this once."

He runs down the stairs and puts the bread and water on the last step before going back up. He sits on the top step and grins as he watches me crawl to the food.

It takes a while, but I make it. With shaking hands, I eat the food so fast that crumbs fall to the floor and water drips down my chin.

I hate myself for wasting the water. The crumbs are not a problem. I can pick them up later. I might not get anything more to drink for a while.

When the cool liquid hits my belly, my baby moves again. Warmth spreads through my chest. Life is still growing inside me.

With renewed energy, I wolf down the food like an animal. Why not? I might as well be an animal trapped inside a cage.

If I had an option, I would save some of the food for later, but that's risky. He might decide to take it away. His changes in mood are unpredictable.

When all the food is gone, including the bread crumbs on the floor, he starts laughing.

"You should see yourself." He shakes his head. "You're pathetic and dirty. No amount of soap and water is enough to scrub you clean. You'll always be a filthy prostitute."

I crawl back to my usual place and lie back down. Responding to him would be a waste of time.

After watching me for a while, he pulls out a lighter and lights a cigarette. He pulls on it like someone who has always smoked. I had no idea he was a smoker. But then again, I married him without really knowing who he really is. I married a stranger. He also married a stranger.

"I have a question." His words come out with the smoke. "Was prison worse than this?"

"No," I say. It's what he wants to hear. I wouldn't want him to think I'm not suffering enough.

"I see." He coughs. "By the way, before you ate, did you take a moment to consider that perhaps the food might be tainted? What if I lied about letting your baby live?"

My blood runs cold. "Oh, my God." I was so hungry that the idea of him poisoning me or my baby never crossed my mind.

While I shove a finger down my throat to get the food to come back up, he laughs out loud and pushes himself to his feet. "Always be careful what you put into your mouth, porcupine." He closes the door and locks it.

I vomit out some of the food with tears and snot mixing together on my face. My hands clutch my stomach, which is cramping more than before. It can't be hunger this time. I'm unsure whether it's brought on by fear or the medication that's meant to kill my baby.

I force myself to throw up until most of the food gushes out.

He must have heard me vomit because the door opens again and his presence fills the room.

"I was messing with you. There was nothing in your food or water. But now that you've wasted food, you're not getting anything more." He slams the door shut again.

A raw, angry scream builds up inside my throat and explodes from my lips.

"I hate you, you monster." I shout, tears running down my cheeks. "You make me sick."

When he doesn't respond, I climb the stairs and slam the closed door with my fists until they hurt. When I still don't get a reaction, I slide to the floor. That's when I hear a whistle and his footsteps as he walks away.

He has forgotten to turn off the light.

He was there the entire time, listening to my rant, enjoying every second of it.

Trembling with fury, I return to the bottom of the stairs and take out my anger on the many boxes in the room. I'm still screaming with frustration as I send boxes crashing to the floor, contents spilling out of them. I continue until I have no energy left. To my surprise, one of the boxes that bursts open is filled with women's clothing.

Observing the mess on the floor, I notice a pink notebook that looks more like a diary. It looks so different from the rest of the stuff on the floor that it stands out.

I pick it up and sit on the floor with it on my lap. I flip open the cover. There's a name.

Alison Creed.

My gut tells me it's her, Jared's former wife. That's if he wasn't lying to me.

I shut the diary again and hold it against my body, afraid to look inside, afraid of what I might discover.

But I need to know the truth. If Alison was his wife, I want to know what happened to her. The same thing could happen to me. I stroke the soft leather for a while until I find the courage to open it.

It *is* a diary. The first entry is written in a smooth handwriting that looks feminine.

May 16, 2006

Dear Diary,

Last week I married Jack. It was the happiest day of my life. Today, I want out. Between our wedding day and today, something changed. He changed. He's not the same man, and I'm not the same woman.

The wedding was my dream, but the marriage is my worst nightmare. My husband hit me for looking at a waiter a few seconds too long. I feel ashamed to be that woman, the one whose husband beats her up.

He apologized, many times. He promised it will never happen again. I don't know if he means it. I don't know if I can forget. This is not what I imagined marriage to be like.

Will he keep his promise? I hope I'm strong enough to wait and find out.

I turn the page for more. I find nothing. It's the one and only entry in the diary. There are white hearts on the spine. Whoever Alison was, my heart aches for her. She must have bought the diary to journal her married life. Maybe she bought it before the wedding, before she discovered the other side to her husband.

The light is switched off while I'm still flicking through the pages. It doesn't matter. I don't need another entry to prove to me that Jared or Jack killed his wife. I could be next.

I need to get out of this basement. I have a plan that could backfire if I fail. But I need to try.

While cleaning up the mess I made, I lose the pieces of wood that were once a photo frame, my weapons. I don't have time to look for them.

I hide the diary in one of the boxes underneath piles of her dresses. For him to keep some of Alison's belongings, he must have loved her in his own twisted way.

After cleaning up, I lie on my side, put my arms around my stomach, and scream at the top of my lungs. I don't stop until the light goes on and the door slams against the wall when he swings it open.

"Shut up." He runs down the stairs to me.

My screams turn to whimpers. I look up to meet his eyes.

"Help me, please. The baby. I think I'm...ouch." I scream out again, eyes tightly shut.

Please God, don't let him see through me.

I'm surprised when he drops to his knees next to me and lays a hand on my body. I do my best not to flinch.

"This is a good thing," he whispers. "It was not meant to be born."

I bite my tongue to prevent myself from saying something scathing and continue to pretend I'm in unbearable pain.

After a few heartbeats, he stands up and goes back up the stairs. He takes two steps at a time.

I'm about to lose hope when he comes back five minutes later with a big bottle of water. He puts it on the floor next to me.

"It's safe to drink." He heads back to the stairs. "Drink the water and wash your face. Tomorrow you can come back upstairs."

CHAPTER 30

I'm awake, but I keep my eyes closed. I don't need to open them to know he's in the basement with me. My nose knows his toxic scent by heart.

I don't remember sleeping. My body doesn't feel rested. But I must have slept for him to sneak in without me hearing him.

I don't move a muscle as I wait for what he's about to do.

He shifts next to me. I grit my teeth when his breath caresses my face.

"Boo," he says and I jump.

My eyes fly open. He has not switched on the light. He obviously wanted to surprise me, but I can see him clearly even in the semidarkness.

"I knew you were awake," he whispers.

He places a hand on my stomach and keeps it there. "It's still alive, isn't it?"

I pretend to be too weak to respond. I'm afraid of what to say. He could punish me if he finds out I was lying to him.

I clear my throat and swallow hard. "I don't know," I say truthfully. Only a medical examination can prove whether my baby is still alive. I haven't felt a movement for a couple of hours now and it scares me to death. Pretending the baby is dead fills me with guilt. What if it really happens? It was a stupid idea that could cost me even my own life.

"I doubt it's alive. You, on the other hand, look like you're on the brink of death."

I breathe a sigh of relief when he withdraws his hand and places it on my forehead. Tears come to my eyes because, for a brief second, I remember the man he used to be, the man I thought he was.

"Jack," I whisper. "Don't hurt me. You're a good person."

"It's me, sweetheart...Jared. Jack is gone."

It's clear to me now that he's suffering from a personality disorder. But I cannot relax. Even though Jack seems to be more evil, there's a dark side to Jared as well. Letting my guard down is out of the question.

"Jared," I say as fresh tears flood my eyes. "You're a good man. That's why I fell in love with you." What I'm saying is garbage. I fell in love with a monster, but I have to tell him what I hope he wants to hear so that maybe I can have a chance at survival.

"Maybe," he says. "I think I am a good

person, but as you already know, there's a dark side to me that comes out sometimes. Once it's out, I cannot control it."

"Jack," I say softly.

"Yeah, that's what I call him." He buries his hands in his hair. "You know, Kelsey, for a while there, I thought you were changing me. I thought I was falling in love with you. I thought I could give up the money and keep you instead. I made you so perfect that I almost forgot what you were."

"You did, Jared. You changed me. I'm not the same person who worked as a stripper. I'm never going back to that life."

He doesn't respond to that. He just glares at me for a long time. Without another word, he pushes his hands underneath my body and gathers me into his arms.

When he walks toward the stairs, I stop myself from crying with relief. I can never let my true emotions show. Jack could return at any time and take over. He could change his mind about taking me upstairs.

I close my eyes, hoping that when I open them again, we will be out of the basement. Even being locked up inside the bedroom is more bearable than being inside a place that brings back so many horrible memories for me.

Instead of taking me to the bedroom, he walks into the upstairs bathroom and lowers me to the thick rug on the floor.

"You need to get cleaned up." He straightens up. "You don't smell good."

I nod because that's all I can do right now. I have to pretend he's right about everything until I prove him wrong.

He kneels down next to me and picks up a strand of my hair, tucking it behind my ear. "It didn't have to be like this, you know." His face folds with what looks like sadness. "All you had to do was obey me. I wanted you to be the perfect wife. I gave you the perfect life to go with it."

"Yes, you did." I blink. "I'm sorry."

"From now on, you will obey me. You will do everything I ask you to do."

"Yes." I lower my lashes to hide the lie. "I'll do whatever you want." I want to ask him to also promise he won't hurt my baby. But neither of us knows whether the baby is still alive. It's best to pretend it doesn't even exist so as not to anger him.

His lips twitch in a smile. Is he wondering whether he can trust me? He'd be a fool to do that. But I won't be surprised if he believes my lies. He's not normal. Something inside him is broken.

"Good." He stands up again and turns on the shower.

While I wash myself, he steps out of the

bathroom, but he doesn't go far.

As the water runs down my body, I tip my head upward, drinking some of it, quenching a thirst that refuses to go away.

The warm water feels so great on my skin that I can't hold back the tears of relief.

I wash my hair with more shampoo than I have ever used before and scrub every inch of my body.

Before I rinse myself off, I run my hand around my stomach, round and round, praying my baby is still inside there, still trusting me to get us out of the dangerous situation.

The unexpected flutter fills me with so much joy I choke up.

I blink back the tears. I can't cry anymore. I don't want to give Jared more satisfaction at seeing me vulnerable.

"Are you done?" he asks from outside the door.

"Almost," I say. After drinking and cleaning myself, I feel better on the inside, but my body is still weak. I'm finding it hard to stand for long, leaning against the wall tiles most of the time for support.

I scrub myself some more, then I step out, my knees threatening to give way. I need food and proper sleep to get my energy back.

I grab a bathrobe from behind the door and put it on. He opens the door to let me out.

The rest of the day almost feels like old times, when I thought I was married to the man of my dreams. He cooks me breakfast, lunch, and even dinner. When night falls, he lies next to me on the bed.

But it's hard to relax. I'm not sure when Jack will return, when the rug will be pulled from underneath me. I have a feeling it won't be long until I'm plunged back into my nightmare.

CHAPTER 31

I wake up with a jolt. I had planned on sleeping with one eye open, but I failed. Sleeping in a comfortable bed again helped me relax more than I wanted to. I'm not sure what time it is, but it's still dark in the room.

My heart is thudding as I listen to the silence.

I don't hear Jared's breathing. I'm not sure if he's still in bed next to me. I'm afraid to reach out and touch him.

I blink to help my eyes get used to the dark. Suddenly, a piercing light cuts through the darkness. Someone is shining a bright yellow light from one end of the room to the bed.

It's him. He's sitting in a chair by the window, watching me.

"How are you feeling?" he asks. His voice is as gentle as it has been the entire day.

How long has he been watching me sleep?

He rises from the chair and comes to the bed, the flashlight still in his hand. He leans down to brush my hair from my face and plants a kiss on my forehead. I swallow down my disgust.

"I hope I didn't wake you," he says. "I loved watching you sleep."

"What time is it?" I attempt to stretch my arms above my head, but something around my left wrist restricts my movements. When I figure out what it is, panic grips me. He has handcuffed me to the bed. "What did you do?"

He switches on the light and comes back to stand in front of me. A dark cloud settles on his features. "You don't really think I trust you, do you? I'm not stupid. I can see in your eyes that if you get the chance to escape again, you will. Am I wrong?"

I yank at my arm as if I have the power to snap the handcuff open without a key. I give up quickly. Trying to release myself from handcuffs will only lead to bruised skin around the wrists. "I won't. I won't do it."

He puts a hand to his heart. "I want to believe you, but I'm sure you understand why I can't do that. When we sleep, you will be handcuffed." He sits on the edge of the bed. "Now that I've made that clear, there's something I want to discuss with you."

I clench my teeth and say nothing.

"Our friends have been wondering when we'll have another dinner party. You know how much they love your food. It hasn't been long since we invited them over, but we should host another dinner again soon. How about in a week's time? Are you up to it?" He rubs his chin, waiting for an answer.

A normal question for normal people. But we're far from normal.

"Yes," I say in a hurry. I'd welcome any opportunity that gets me out of the room and around people. During a dinner, people will be coming and going, which means the front door will be open. I have to find a way to sneak out the door while he's distracted by all the conversations.

If I don't make it out of the door, I'll be forced to confide in one of the guests. I can't miss the opportunity to tell someone that Jared is keeping me captive. I'll beg the person to call the cops. When they arrive to take him away, I'll run before he tells the cops who I am and what I'm hiding. I'm pretty sure they will not believe him right away or at all.

"Perfect." He taps his fingers against his lips. "I'll do the grocery shopping on that day and you will create one of your beautiful meals. I already look forward to it."

"Yeah. Me too." That day will change everything. Either I will be free from him, or end up dead. If he doesn't kill me, I'll be severely punished for trying to get away.

He studies me for a long time again and when

I think he will say something, he switches off the light and leaves the room. He doesn't lock the door. He doesn't need to. I'm not going anywhere.

I want to scream for him to come back and release me, but it's best not to annoy him. Feeling trapped but also hopeful, I lie back on the bed and stare up at the dark ceiling. Maybe I should force myself to go back to sleep, but my bladder is starting to complain. Ignoring the uncomfortable sensation only makes it stronger.

"Jared," I call, praying he's not in a bad mood again. "I need to go to the bathroom."

I call for him several more times. He doesn't respond.

It feels like an hour until he finally comes to the room. He finds me on the verge of peeing myself.

"What do you want?" he asks, irritated. "I was watching a movie."

"I'm sorry." I press my legs tightly together. "I need to go to the bathroom…please?"

"Fine," he says, but he doesn't approach the bed.

"Please, Jared. I need to go. I won't do anything stupid."

"You better not." He reaches into his pocket and pulls out a silver key.

"Thank you," I murmur when I'm free of the handcuffs.

"You're welcome." He helps me to my feet and escorts me to the bathroom, waiting outside the door until I'm done.

"You're doing well," he says when he tucks me back in bed and handcuffs me again. "As long as you behave, you never have to fear me. When you misbehave, the only person you hurt is yourself. I'll be right back."

He disappears from the room for five minutes. When he walks back through the door, he's holding a cup in one hand and a book in the other.

"This is for you." He places the cup in my hands. It's filled with warm milk. I lift it to my lips and take a sip, then another. It tastes so good that I don't stop until it's gone.

Taking it from me, Jared puts it on the floor because there's no nightstand in the room anymore.

He sits down next to me on the bed, still holding the book he brought with him. It's my cookbook. He bought it for me a few days after we got married.

"I figured that since we both can't sleep, how about we pick something out for the dinner? I'm so excited I cannot wait."

He places the book on my lap, but it's him who flips through it. I've cooked most of the recipes, but he's able to find several he hasn't tasted yet.

"How about this for dessert?" He points at a chocolate and peanut butter pudding pie.

I nod. Whatever he chooses is fine with me. The food is not my focus.

He looks satisfied as he continues to flip through the pages. "For the main course, let's do seared scallops with brown butter and lemon juice sauce. This looks delicious." He runs a finger down the recipe page. "I'm sure everyone will love it."

It's amazing how he manages to look normal, not like someone who killed his pregnant wife. He's so sick, I can't figure out whether he belongs in prison or a mental institution.

"Looks good," I murmur, ignoring the sick feeling in the pit of my stomach.

"Why do I get the feeling that you're not that excited?"

"I am." I sit up straight. "I'm just...I'm tired, that's all."

"Yeah, it's after midnight. Sorry about that. The dinner party will be our last. We have to make it one we will always remember. Everything should be perfect, including the decorations."

I stiffen inside. I want to ask him why he claims it's the last dinner party. Is it because he plans to get rid of me after that?

It's a good thing he let the little bit of information slip. Now I'm even more motivated to make sure I get away as soon as the opportunity presents itself.

He takes the book from me and snaps it shut, holding it to his chest. "I know I said we should do it in a week, but why not sooner? Next weekend? That gives us three days to plan."

I only have three days to plan my escape? I don't know whether it's enough. I don't know whether any amount of time would be enough. I don't even know exactly how I'm going to get away. I might not even come up with a plan until the weekend.

As much as having only three days to come up with a plan makes me nervous, a flicker of excitement also courses through me. In three days, if I'm lucky, it will all be over.

"It's perfect," I say. I do my best to keep myself from giving anything away.

Satisfied, Jared switches the light off and closes the door. He slides into bed next to me.

I keep my eyes closed the entire night, but I don't sleep a wink.

CHAPTER 32

The day of the dinner party, Jared keeps me locked up the entire morning and afternoon.

Instead of being terrified about how the day will end, there's a fire burning inside me. I still don't have a concrete plan of escape, but I won't be spending another night in Jared's house. I will not be locked away and handcuffed like a prisoner. I'm tired of fighting for my life, for my sanity, for my freedom.

I hear Jared's whistling before he enters the room and unlocks the handcuffs. Torturing me must be good for his mood. He has on a white polo shirt and beige shorts, and his hair is glistening in the light that floods the room through the window. He looks like an angel, but we both know what he truly is.

"Are you ready to have fun tonight?" He kisses me on the forehead. The touch of his lips leaves goosebumps on my skin brought on by disgust instead of desire.

"I am." I don't say another word as he leads me to the bathroom to brush my teeth and wash my face. He didn't allow me to do it in the morning.

Inside the kitchen, all the ingredients are laid out on the counter.

"Everything you need is there." He waves a hand over the food, proud of himself. "If you need anything else, say the word." He drops into a chair at the kitchen table and plants his elbows on the surface, his chin rested on his fists. He watches me standing in the middle of the kitchen, trying to decide what part of the meal to start with.

"You better start cooking. It's already six. The guests will be here in two hours."

Even though I was brave for most of the day, I'm suddenly nervous. What if I fail? What if I end up in prison instead of him?

"Do you mind if I use the bathroom?" I ask.

"Why?" He frowns. "You just went to the bathroom upstairs."

"I'm sorry. I need to...I need to pee again." My need to urinate has little to do with the pregnancy and more to do with the terror that's loosening my bladder.

"All right. But hurry." Instead of allowing me to go alone, he leads me through the door, his hand pressed to my lower back.

He takes me to the guest bathroom and waits

for me outside. He leaves the door open.

I lower myself onto the toilet and close my eyes, focusing on the baby inside of me. I felt it move again this morning. I have to fight for him or her.

If it weren't for my baby, I would have given up long ago. Jared would have broken me completely. It's the baby that helped me make it through each day without going crazy.

Feeling stronger, I rise from the toilet and flush even though I didn't actually use it. When I turn to wash my hands, I notice for the first time that the mirror that used to hang above the sink is gone. He removed it, like he removed the one upstairs.

I shrug. I don't need to see myself in the mirror to notice the hollows in my cheeks or the bags underneath my eyes.

I run cold water over my hands and press my cool fingertips against my eyes.

"You look tired," he says from behind me. "But it's nothing makeup can't hide. Like always, the guests will admire your beauty as much as your food."

I don't say anything. His compliments mean nothing to me.

"I'm ready to start cooking," I say. He nods and escorts me back to the kitchen.

He watches my every move, his gaze following me around the kitchen, even when he pretends to be reading the paper. He only helps me when there's something that needs cutting. I'm not allowed to touch the only knife left in the kitchen. He's the one who slices the lemons in half for the scallop sauce and the onions for the French onion soup.

If someone were looking in from outside, they would think we are a normal couple preparing dinner together. They would think Jared is the perfect husband and I'm the perfect wife. They would have no idea that we are living the perfect lie.

"You're lucky, you know," he says, glancing up from the paper.

"What do you mean?" I turn away from the stainless-steel skillet, which I have already coated with oil, ready to cook the scallops. The whole time I keep thinking it would be the perfect weapon to attack him with. But I remind myself that physically attacking him might lead to me getting hurt, especially since he has a knife right next to him.

"What I'm saying is that you're lucky that the cops have not come sniffing around again. I told them we were both home the night Victor was murdered. They wanted to speak to you, but I told them my pregnant wife was too sick to speak to anyone." He looks back down at the newspaper. "I'm actually surprised they haven't returned. They must have someone else on their radar, possibly someone from outside."

"Yeah." I turn back to the skillet and switch on the stove, heating it up until wisps of smoke curl up toward my face. I can feel him watching me, but I don't turn around. I place the scallops in the hot skillet one by one.

I guess he was trying to remind me that I'm still at his mercy so I don't betray him tonight.

"Will you not thank me?" he asks. "I expected you to be grateful that I've been working so hard to cover up your tracks."

"Thank you," I say. Instead of looking at him, I approach the fridge, not even sure what I'm getting. I pull the handle and realize with a sinking feeling that it's locked.

"Ooops," he says. "I'm sorry about that." He walks up next to me and unlocks the fridge.

I take out random things. I'm no longer focusing on the recipe. I don't care how the meal turns out. I'm just waiting for the time when I can get away.

I return to the stove and watch the scallops cook until they're golden brown, then I turn them over.

I continue to cook all the dishes with Jared looking over my shoulder. His gaze makes my skin itch. The desire to claw his eyes out steals my breath.

I manage to cook food that he's pleased with. The past few days, I was allowed to eat more than bread and water, and tonight I'm allowed to taste the food. Even though I'm distracted, it tastes pretty good.

"The guests will be here in half an hour. You should go and clean yourself up," he says, getting rid of the knife and anything else he thinks I could use to attack him with. "Make yourself pretty."

He follows me to the bathroom. Since he doesn't leave the room, I decide not to take a shower. It makes me uncomfortable to have him watching me shower when we are no longer husband and wife, except on paper. I'm also nervous about him staring at my stomach. He might figure out that the baby is still alive.

I approach the sink and splash my face with water. My skin instantly feels rejuvenated again. I also wipe away the sweat under my armpits.

"Why don't you shower or take a bath?" he asks, perching on the edge of the bathtub.

"There's not much time left. I want to take my time with the makeup." I chew a corner of my lip. "I have a pocket mirror inside my handbag. Do you mind if I use it?"

"Of course not. I want you to look your best." He leaves the bathroom to get me the handbag. When I start to enjoy the few seconds without him around, he returns.

He rummages inside my bag until he finds the mirror and hands it to me. I thank him and apply my makeup while sitting on the closed toilet lid, the mirror perched on my lap.

I take my time sliding the mascara wand over my already long lashes, smearing concealer over anything I want to hide, and dabbing tinted lip gloss over my lips.

"You did a great job," he says, peering at my face. "Now you need to get dressed."

We go to the bedroom together.

A silver and black dress is draped over the bed.

"It's for you," he says. "You've been so good the past couple of days. You need to be rewarded. You'll look beautiful in it."

"Thank you, Jared." I pick up the dress and pull it over my head, facing away from him.

"You look stunning," he says when I turn around again. "You're the perfect host."

I force my lips to smile. The dress is beautiful, but I'm nervous when he hands me a pair of silver high heels. There's no way I'll be able to run in them. I guess I'll have to do it barefoot.

"That dress belonged to my ex-wife, Alison."

I sink onto the bed, glaring at him. "I don't want to wear it." He's sick to think I would want to wear a dress that belonged to the woman he murdered.

When I attempt to lift it over my head again, he grabs my wrist.

"It's just a dress," he says through clenched

teeth. "And it looks good on you. You're wearing it tonight."

"Okay," I say after a long pause. I have to be careful. I need to do what he says or he might cancel the dinner.

Shortly before eight, Jared follows me to the kitchen, even though he hasn't changed his clothes.

Trying not to think about the dress I'm wearing, I turn on the stove to heat up the soup.

At five minutes to eight, the guests still haven't arrived. It's weird because they're never late. Especially Linda, who sometimes comes way too early.

"I guess they're running late," Jared says. "We should get started without them."

"Start eating?" My brow draws together. "Without them?"

"Yes. I hate it when people are late. It shows disrespect."

I find it strange, but I follow his lead. I have no other choice. I'm sure the guests will be horrified when they arrive to find their hosts have already started dinner without them. But it's Jared's house. It's Jared's rules. I hope they will arrive soon.

I scoop the hot soup into a large bowl and carry it to the dining room. When I reach the doorway, I come to a halt.

Jared had been responsible for decorating the

dining room. The table is laid and everything looks great except for one thing that makes my stomach turn.

The chairs around the table are not empty. But instead of people, life-sized female dolls are seated in them, slumping forward because they are unable to remain straight.

Only two chairs are empty – mine and Jared's.

"Looks like the guests have arrived after all," Jared says, pointing to a blonde doll with bright blue eyes.

I can feel my face losing color. I can't even find words to say to him.

"You should see your face right now." He starts laughing. When he's done, his expression grows serious. "I know you were looking forward to this day, but I can't let anyone see you in this state. I lied upstairs. The makeup didn't do a good job. You look tired and unhappy. Our friends might ask questions, especially after what you did at the festival." He waves at the table. "But since these guests cannot speak, they're perfect for us. Come on, this will be a dinner party to remember."

"You're sick." I move forward until I sink into one of the empty chairs, devastated that my plans of escape have come crashing down.

He sits down in his chair. "You should stop talking that way. It upsets me. I've been so good to you the past few days. Tonight, I'm allowing you to eat great food. You should be grateful."

I don't know how it happens. I don't know where I find the courage, but one second I'm paralyzed by rage, and the next I'm on my feet, hurling the hot bowl of soup in his direction. He roars when the bowl catches the side of his face and hot soup pours over him, staining his polo shirt brown.

He rises from the table like an angry lion. I'm too far from the door to run for it, so I kick off my shoes and grab one of them. When he lunges for me, the heel connects with his forehead.

Roaring with rage, he grabs it from me and tosses it away. While he tries to recover from the pain, I take my chances and run from the dining room.

Instead of the front door, which I'm sure is still locked, I run to the guest bathroom. I slam the door shut and lean against it, dizzy with fear.

"We're done," he shouts from the other side. Every word is like poison. "Game over."

The bathroom window is too small for me to climb out of, but I still open it and scream for help.

CHAPTER 33

Game over.

The two words penetrate my mind and my entire body, sucking the air out of my lungs, dashing any hopes of escape I might have had. Panic riots through me.

Running into the bathroom might not have been a good idea. Maybe I should have tried the front door. What if it was not locked?

Each time Jared's fists bang against the wooden door, I jump. What if he kicks it down?

This can't be it. This cannot be how my life ends.

There has to be a way I can escape from the house without him hurting me or the baby. The murderous look on his face when I attacked him sends shivers down my spine.

"You've gone too far." His voice cuts through the wood and slices through my heart. "It's easier to get rid of you once and for all. Since you will be my wife at the time of death, I'll still be able to get my money." He hammers against the door again. "Maybe I'll use it to move away from this boring little town and start a new life someplace else, with a good woman."

My fingers curl around my throat. My breath feels as though it's been cut off. Tears trickle down my cheeks when I think I could be Jared's next victim. He's done it before, murdered his wife and unborn child. He got away with it. What will stop him from doing it again?

I crouch in a corner of the bathroom, scanning the small room for something I can use to defend myself. The idea of Jared going out into the world again and living without remorse fills my stomach with acid.

He needs to be stopped. Maybe the only way I can stop him is by putting my own freedom at risk. If I make it out alive, I might have to turn myself in and confess to Victor's murder. I have to overcome my fear of prison. It's safer than inside Jared's house. The baby and I will find a way to survive behind bars.

I clasp my hands tightly in my lap and make myself a promise. If I go down, Jared will go down with me. I will not let him get away with murder again, even if I have to pay a high price for it.

I rise up from the floor and return to the window. Last time I screamed until my throat was sore, but I have to try again in case someone hears me this time. It surprises me that no one has come to my rescue yet. It's the middle of the night and a woman is screaming. Why has no one called 911?

I call for help again until I run out of breath and give in to a coughing fit. Drained, I slump against the wall. This is not getting me anywhere. I need to gather my strength, to think clearly.

It could be that someone heard me and called the cops. But I need to come up with Plan B, in case no one is coming to help me.

Squeezing my eyes tight, I force myself to think of a way out. Even though the front door might be locked, there might be other ways to escape.

If I make it out of the bathroom, my only way out of the house might be the kitchen. It's the closest room to the bathroom. It also has a window large enough for me to fit through.

When he starts kicking against the door or perhaps striking it with a hard object, I search frantically for something to attack him with.

"Don't think I can't break this door down," he shouts. Something hard crashes against the door.

Biting my lower lip, I grab the first object my fingers touch, a heavy ceramic flowerpot from the windowsill. If I hit him over the head with it, I might be able to knock him down.

My fingers are shaking so hard and the sweat

coating the palms of my hands makes it hard for me to hold the pot firmly. I wipe my palms with a towel and grab the pot again, lifting it high above my head as I position myself on one side of the door, ready to attack.

He continues to rage and throw things at the door. Each time I think he will burst right through it, but it's a strong door and it refuses to give in.

When he doesn't get what he wants, he curses a few times, then silence follows.

A few heartbeats later, I hear him talking as though to someone else. He must be standing a good distance from the door because I cannot make out the words he's saying. Maybe he's talking to himself.

He stops talking, but his feet continue to pace around the door as he waits for me like a hunter waiting for its prey.

Between the thudding of my heart and the rush in my ears, I catch the sound of the doorbell ringing.

Relief like I've never known before gushes through me. Someone must have heard me scream and called the cops.

The longer the doorbell rings, the faster my hope dies. Jared is refusing to go to the door.

My stomach drops.

Even if he does answer the door, he could tell whoever is out there lies about me and they might go away. Maybe he'll say I'm crazy. After the way I acted at the festival in front of many witnesses, the person would probably believe him.

Even though the bathroom window doesn't face the front of the house, I scream out again in the hopes that the person at the door will hear me.

The doorbell stops ringing for a few seconds only to start all over again. The sound is unbroken, which means the person at the door is holding down the button. The sound is soon followed by the thud of Jared's footsteps as he finally walks away from the door.

I thought he was smarter than that. If I were him, I would never have left.

My chance has finally come. I unlock and open the door carefully, cringing when it pushes against broken furniture. I step through it and close it again. I want him to think I'm still inside.

Without wasting time, I run on tiptoes down the hall in the direction of the kitchen.

The kitchen door is wide open. As soon as I enter, something pierces my right foot. It's a wood splinter. I pause to yank it out.

The pain burns through my skin, but I clench my teeth tight so I don't scream. I can't mess up my chance to escape.

I consider closing the door, but it won't be a good idea. He will walk past the kitchen on his way back to the bathroom and know immediately that I'm inside.

Instead, I hurry to the back door and push the handle down. Of course, it's not open. Before I can recover from my disappointment, I hear the jingle of keys. I spin around, my hair flinging itself across my face. My vision is only disturbed for a moment before I see Jared standing by the door, closing it. A twisted sneer splits his face.

"You should know by now that I'm always one step ahead," he says, locking the door. We're both trapped inside now.

I fell right into his trap.

"Don't kill me." I hate for him to see my fear, but I can't stop my body from shaking out of control.

"I'm afraid it's the only way out of this mess." He uses the back of his hand to wipe the sweat from his bloody forehead. "You messed everything up, Kelsey. I gave you a chance and you blew it." He narrows his eyes. "I'm a patient man, but you are much more trouble than I can handle."

I swallow my fears and toss my hands into the air. Anger burns the back of my throat. "Fine, Jared. I'm tired. Go ahead. Kill me. Murder me like you murdered your first wife. At least I'll be dead and at peace, and you'll be running from the law forever. You will never find peace because you'll always be afraid to get caught. I'm talking from experience." I shrug. "So, go ahead. Do it."

Laughing, he bends to lift something off the floor, a large plastic container filled with clear liquid.

When I read the blue label on the container, I choke back a cry and my earlier courage comes crashing down.

Gasoline.

CHAPTER 34

His tight expression tells me everything I need to know. There's no going back. He intends to set me on fire and get away with murder.

The man who puts out fires for a living is about to set a deadly one.

If I had any doubts that he's a heartless psychopath, those doubts are now null and void. The flames of his anger are already burning. There's no physical fire yet, but I already feel the heat on my skin.

"You really want to do this?" Keeping him talking delays the inevitable. It gives me a chance to get used to the idea of being burned to death.

"You give me no choice." He drops the bundle of keys into his pocket. "Your time is up. It ends here...for you."

My gaze flickers to the fire alarm high above his head. It's broken. He planned everything.

With a sick grin on his face, he unscrews the cap on the container. I have no idea whether it's my imagination, but I already smell the dangerous liquid.

I should keep him talking, but I have no idea what more to say to him. How does one communicate with a monster?

There's nothing I can do to save myself, and the person who was ringing the doorbell is long gone and probably won't return.

When my fighting spirit deserts me and I start to accept my fate, I remember my baby. I no longer care about my own life, but my baby's life depends on mine. I search my mind for one last thing I can do to save us both.

An idea drops into my mind without warning.

The kitchen is mine. It's where I've spent most of my time when Jared and I were married. I know it better than he does. He's holding a container of gasoline, but there are other flammable substances in the kitchen. I'm standing in front of a cabinet filled with them.

His eyes never leave mine as he lifts the container and starts spilling its contents all over the place. As the liquid lands on my skin and slides across the floor, I take a few steps back until my back comes into contact with the long cabinet where all the oils and spices are kept.

I'm about to turn and open it when in the corner of my eye, I notice the large bottle of oil I forgot to put back in the cabinet after I cooked the scallops. Before fear can stop me, I grab it with both hands.

"What do you think you're doing?" He stops pouring the gasoline, but continues to hold the container.

"If I'm burning down, so are you." As our eyes lock, I swing back my hand and hurl the bottle in his direction, aimed at his head, which is still bleeding from the wounds I had inflicted earlier. His skin is red from being scalded by the hot soup.

He ducks at the last second. The bottle flies past him to explode against the wall behind him, sending shards of glass and oil flying in all directions. Some of the oil lands on him.

Furious, he attempts to charge toward me, perhaps to kill me with his bare hands, but he slips on the oil and stumbles. I turn back to snatch another bottle of oil from the cabinet while he has lost his balance. When I turn back to him, I choke back a cry. He has straightened up again and he's holding a lighter. His eyes on mine, he flicks it on and extends his hand in my direction, as far away from his body as possible.

"Once I throw this at you, you'll burn to a crisp."

He's right. There's enough gasoline on me, the smell strong as it floods my lungs, poisoning my baby.

"You and me both." I'm not ready to give up yet. I grit my teeth and send the second bottle of oil flying across the room. Like the last time, he ducks out of the way. I don't stop. I grab the skillet from the stove.

This time, I hit him on the head and he yells out. He drops the lighter on the floor, where the small flame instantly catches the oil and gasoline and explodes into bigger flames around him. His eyes widen in horror.

As the fire starts to spread across the kitchen, I know it's only a matter of seconds before I'm engulfed.

While Jared stumbles across the kitchen, bumping into chairs and sending them crashing to the floor, I try to find a way out.

Since the key to the kitchen door is inside his pocket, I have no choice but to find another way out.

Holding my breath so I don't inhale too much smoke, I grab a chair and slam it against the kitchen window above the sink. I must not have hit hard enough because it comes bouncing back, leaving only a crack.

I try again, screaming at the same time the chair connects with the glass, breaking right through it. The sounds of glass exploding and my own screams merge with Jared's roars of pain. He's rolling on the floor now, trying to extinguish the fire.

I peel my gaze from him. With the help of the chair, I climb over the sink and push myself through the window. The glass slices my skin, but I don't care. I don't have time to give pain my full attention.

The flames are already starting to lick their way up the kitchen curtains.

I make it out alive, falling on my back in the garden. Pain explodes inside my stomach. I try to scream, but only release whimpers.

An arm around my stomach, I scramble to my feet and run across the garden toward the fence that separates our house from Rachel's.

The fence is short enough for me to clamber over, and the adrenaline inside me makes the task easier than it would normally be. But there are rosebushes on the other side. I land right in them, the thorns piercing my body. More pain flares across my skin. But I'm alive.

By the time I reach Rachel's front door, my lungs are burning and I'm gasping for air.

I alternate between ringing the bell and knocking on the door.

The lights go on inside, but she doesn't open the door immediately.

Someone must have called the police because I can hear the sound of sirens in the distance. It's like in the movies. Many times, the cops arrive when it's all over.

I knock again until my knuckles burn. When the door is finally swung open, I almost fall inside because I was leaning heavily against it.

"Kelsey?" Rachel says, tightening the belt of her bathrobe. "What are you doing here? What happened?"

I don't understand why she's asking. She only needs to look out the window to see smoke pouring out of the house I used to call my home.

"Fire...Jared." One of my hands is still around my stomach and the other is pointing toward the house. "My baby."

Rachel steps out onto the porch. When she sees the fire, her hand goes to her mouth. "Oh, my God. What did you do?"

I consider telling her everything that happened, but I don't even know where to start. I'm also in so much pain that all I want to do is lie down. Surely, she sees how hurt I am.

"Help me," I cough out the words. I try to say something else, but my body gives up on me. I cannot stop myself from crumbling to the floor of her porch.

Rachel kneels in front of me and brushes my wild hair away from my face.

"Don't worry," she whispers into my ear. "The cops will be here soon." Instead of helping me inside, she gets to her feet and lowers herself onto the porch swing. Through the blur in my eyes, I watch her swing back and forth, making me dizzy.

The sirens get louder, but I'm starting to drift in and out of consciousness.

"Hang in there," Rachel says from a distance. "You'll be fine." But she doesn't come to help me.

It feels like an eternity until the cops and paramedics arrive.

I close my eyes as someone grabs me under the arms and lifts me from the porch.

"She's pregnant," a woman says while I'm being lifted onto a stretcher and an oxygen mask is put around my face.

"Yes, with my husband's baby." Even though my eyes are closed, Rachel's voice is clear enough for me to hear. "She's a murderer. She killed my husband and set her own house on fire. Her husband is inside. She tried to kill him too."

Her words hit me like a bucket of cold water. How long has she known that I'm connected to Victor's death?

The question follows me to the ambulance. As I'm lifted into the back, my eyes drift open in time to see Rachel standing outside, her arms around her body, a smirk on her face.

I don't remember the journey to the hospital. When we arrive, I'm still weak and barely able to speak. Doctors and nurses fuss over me, cleaning and covering up my wounds, checking my vitals, and asking if I can hear them. I hear all their questions, but my ability to speak is lost.

It's only a while later when things calm down, and a new doctor comes to check up on me that

I find my voice again. I have many questions, but only one is more important right now.

"My baby," I croak, my throat still raw from the smoke. "How's my baby?"

The doctor, a woman with a mop of curly hair, looks down on me with a sad expression on her face. She doesn't need to say a word. I already know.

"I'm sorry," she says. "We couldn't hear the heartbeat."

A hot tear slides down the side of my face and drips into my ear.

Jared won. He got what he wanted. The baby is gone and I'll probably end up in prison. If they are able to prove that I killed Victor, I will be put away for two murders—my grandmother's and Victor's. If Jared dies, I might also be blamed for his death.

I close my eyes and Rachel's face shows up behind my eyelids. How did she know? Did Jared tell her? If she knew all this time, why did she not go to the cops?

I need answers, but I'm too overcome with grief at the loss of my baby that all I can do is cry. The hospital staff do their best to comfort me. I push them away. I don't want anyone near me. I don't trust anyone.

After a while, I turn to my side and peer through the glass separating my room from the hallway. A police officer is standing outside in full uniform. They have come to get me.

Overcome with fear of going back to prison, I thrash on the bed, screaming things that don't even make sense. Nurses run into the room and try to hold me down, but they fail.

Left with no other choice, they inject me with something to calm me down. Every muscle in my body relaxes and I fall into the darkness of sleep.

CHAPTER 35

When I wake up, my whole body is in pain. I remember what happened. I lost my baby. I went through hell to save him or her and failed.

Was it because I inhaled too much smoke? Was it the fall? Or was it the fear that killed my baby? I'm not even sure I want to know. It would torture me for the rest of my life.

My hands go to my stomach. It's still bulging out. My baby is still inside me…dead. Grief like I have never experienced before tears through me.

"Mrs. Bloom," a woman says. I blink in surprise. I thought I was alone in the room with the beeping machines. It's hard to see her face through the film of moisture in my eyes.

"That's not my name," I say, turning away from her. "I'm Kel…I'm Kelsey." I don't want anything to attach me to Jared ever again.

"Kelsey," she says as she approaches the bed with a white clipboard. "I'm Dr. Sanders. We saw each other briefly before you fell asleep. How are you feeling? Do you know what happened?"

I know exactly what happened, but it's too painful to put into words, so I say nothing.

"Kelsey, can you hear me?"

I blink and still don't respond. I put my arms around my stomach and continue to stare through the window on one side of the room. The cops are still out there. They don't even scare me anymore.

The doctor gives up and goes to study one of the machines attached to me.

A nurse enters the room. They talk to each other in low voices while I pretend to be asleep.

I hear everything they say to each other.

"She's not communicating. She might need a while before we tell her about the D&C."

"That's a good idea," the nurse whispers. Her voice is slightly deeper than that of Dr. Sanders. "The cops are still waiting to question her."

My arms tighten around my belly. From movies I've watched in the past, I know they're planning to perform a dilation and curettage scraping of my uterine lining.

Tears trickle down my cheeks and sink into the pillow. My life is over. They will remove my baby from my womb and I'll be taken to prison.

"I told them to wait a while," Dr. Sanders responds. "In the state she's in, I doubt she'll speak to them."

She's right. I won't speak to the cops or anyone else. I wish they would all go away. I want to be alone, to say goodbye to my baby. But the cops see me as a criminal, a murderer. It's only a matter of time before they come in.

I open my eyes when the door is opened. Dr. Sanders is leaving.

"Look at you. You're awake. I'm Nurse Julie. That's what everyone around here calls me." The nurse smiles down at me. When another tear rolls down my cheek, she wipes it away with a corner of the bed sheet. "I'm sorry about your baby, love. But you're lucky to be alive. We will take great care of you."

Even though in my mind I'm nodding, my head doesn't move.

Something about the older woman makes me trust her. Maybe it's the faint lines of laughter around her small mouth and almond-shaped eyes.

"Do you know where you are?"

This time, instead of ignoring the question, I manage a reply. "Yes."

"Good. That's really good." She drops into the chair next to my bed. "Do you know what happened?"

Do they have a list of the same questions somewhere that they have to ask patients?

I look away. My gaze meets that of one of the police officers on the other side of the glass. I return my attention back to the nurse. Maybe if I tell her everything, she will try to convince them of my innocence.

"My husband...he tried to kill me." I wet my lower lip. "It was self-defense."

She hands me a plastic cup of water and helps me drink. "Let's not talk about that now," she says when I lie back down. She glances at the cops. "Once you're better, you'll have the chance to tell the police everything, okay?"

An invisible heavy weight presses down on my chest. She's not on my side. She's only doing her job. Overcome with disappointment, I close my eyes again to shut her out. Not long after, I fall asleep.

When I wake up, Dr. Sanders returns to explain the D&C procedure to me. I agree to it without showing any emotion.

The procedure is carried out within two hours.

The next morning, one of the cops is allowed into my room to question me, a wiry man with black hair slicked back with too much gel and thick sideburns. He introduces himself as Officer Rogers. I don't care what his name is.

He asks politely if he can ask me some questions. When I don't give him an answer, he takes a seat next to my bed anyway, and watches me for a long time. Does he think I look like a murderer?

"Mrs. Bloom, can you describe to me exactly what happened at your house last night?"

I'm sure they already have enough evidence to nail me, but they need to know the truth, my side of the story.

"My husband...Jared Bloom." I swallow through my tight throat. "He kept me prisoner in the house for a few weeks. He threatened to kill me and my baby."

I tell the cop about what happened the night I bumped into Victor at the lake. I tell him about Jared and Victor's bet. I tell him about Jared wanting to set me on fire. I leave out the part that exposes me as a fugitive. I can't bring myself to tell him that I'm already wanted for murder.

The officer scribbles my words in his notepad and looks up. His expression gives nothing away. I hate not knowing if he believes me or not. "Okay." He rubs his forehead. "Mrs. Bloom, I'm sure you understand the severity of the situation. I'm afraid that after you are released, you will have to be taken to—"

"It was self-defense." My voice is smothered by tears. "Both times."

He gets up from his chair. "I always believe that evidence speaks louder than words, Mrs. Bloom. An investigation is being carried out as we speak." He walks to the door.

"Is he..." I chew the inside of my mouth. "Did Jared survive?"

With the question comes the memories of what happened in my kitchen, Jared's dangerous words, the smell of gasoline, the heat of the fire. The pain inside and outside my body flares up. They may have treated the wounds and cuts, but the scars will remain forever. Especially the ones carved into my heart. I'll always remember the most terrifying night of my life.

The officer nods. "But he was severely burned. He's in critical condition. We don't know more than that."

"Don't let him get away," I plead, trying to sit up. Pain stops me. "He'll hurt someone else. He killed his wife. Jared murdered his first wife. Before he moved to Sanlow, he was named Jack Creed. Her name was Alison. Please, don't let him get away." I'm not only terrified for his next victim, I'm terrified for my own life. I won't feel safe from him even if I go to prison.

The cop pulls out his notepad again and scribbles down a few words. "We'll have to look into it. I'll be back if I have more questions."

Of course, he will be back. While digging into Jared's past, he might decide to dig into mine. We both have secrets no one else knows about.

Officer Rogers steps out the door only to return again as if he forgot something. "There's something I don't understand," he says, walking back into the room. He doesn't sit this time.

I frown in response.

"You said Victor Hanes raped you. Is that right?"

I take a breath. "He did. The baby I was carrying…it was his." I cough remnants of smoke from my lungs.

"Then why didn't you report the rape?"

"I don't know. I was scared and ashamed." I have to be careful. I haven't told him that Victor knew about my past. "I wasn't thinking straight."

"And why would you want to keep your rapist's baby?"

"Because it was my baby, too." My fingers curl around the sheets. "You don't believe me, do you?"

He sighs and moves back to the door. "I knew Victor Hanes. We played golf together. He was a good man."

That's the wrong thing for him to say. He's a police officer. He's not supposed to rely on his own emotions. He should be impartial and look at both sides of the story.

If he doesn't believe me, no one else will. Everyone in the town of Sanlow who knew and loved Victor will be against me. It's exactly what happened when my grandmother died. It's déjà vu all over again.

Without saying another word, the officer walks out of the room and positions himself next to his partner. As they speak to each other, both turn to peer at me through the glass. When

Officer Rogers pulls out a phone and presses it to his ear, I look away. My story is about to go viral.

In the future, when people talk about murderers, my name will come up. They will refer to me as a serial killer. They might even create documentary films about me. I will go down in history for being a heartless murderer and Jared, the true monster, will probably get away.

I'm not sure if I'm strong enough to handle the unbearable pain I'm sure is about to come my way.

CHAPTER 36

A familiar voice wakes me from a troubled sleep. A flicker of apprehension trickles down my spine.

Rachel is standing in the doorway, watching me through a hooded gaze.

Why is she here?

It's late at night and I don't think I'm allowed to have visitors. But as the widow of the man I'm accused of murdering, she probably has special rights, especially since Officer Rogers used to be Victor's friend.

"Kelsey Bloom," she says, stepping closer into the room. "Surprised to see me?"

I sit up in bed, glancing past her shoulders to the glass partition. The officers are not making a move to remove her from the room, which only confirms that she gets special treatment.

"Hi, Rachel," I say in a suffocated whisper. If only I had known she was coming. I would have thought of something to say to her. I thought the only time I might see her is in court.

Rachel seems different from the woman I've come to know for the past few years. Even though she's dressed all in black, there's a confidence to the way her eyes meet mine. She's also standing taller.

I don't blame her. The woman who killed her husband is about to be brought to justice.

"I didn't plan on coming," she says, pulling up a chair and lowering herself into it. She crosses her legs and smooths out her pleated skirt. "But I needed to see your suffering up close."

"I'm sorry, Rachel." My nose wrinkles when the scent of her sweet, flowery perfume tickles my nostrils. "I'm so sorry about everything."

"For what exactly?" Her perfectly plucked eyebrows draw together to form a deep line in the center of her pale face. "For killing my husband or for lying to me about it?"

"I didn't...look, I didn't mean to kill him. He raped me, Rachel." I stretch out my right leg to release a cramp in my calf. "You told the cops that you saw a video of..." My voice drifts off. "You must have seen him attack me."

Rachel's shoulders curl forward and her chin hits her chest. For a second she reminds me of the insecure woman I knew. She stays like that for a while. When she looks up to meet my gaze again, her eyes have a haunted look to them. "The only thing I saw was you underneath my husband. I also saw you kill him."

She only saw the part of the video Jared wanted her to see. What if there's no full video and Jared had only recorded the part where I hit Victor over the head and ran?

When I mentioned the video to Officer Rogers, he mentioned the cops were not able to locate it anywhere in the house.

"You might not want to hear it, but your husband raped me. I wanted to get him off me. I wanted it to stop. I didn't plan on—"

"You didn't plan on murdering him?" Rachel jumps to her feet and paces the room for a few heartbeats, her mouth working as though she's murmuring something to herself. She returns to the bed and hovers over me, making me feel small.

"I may look stupid, but I'm not blind. I saw how you acted around him, flirting shamelessly in front of me and your own husband. I bet all those dinners you hosted were for his benefit. You loved all the compliments he showered on you about the perfect meals you cooked."

Perfect. There's that ugly word again. It suddenly dawns on me that when we were at the festival, she already knew about what happened between me and Victor. That's the reason why she made those comments about the pains of pregnancy making me less perfect. But how long has she known?

"That's not true," I say, my own anger surging through me. "Come on, Rachel. Surely, you are smarter than that. I'm sure you were aware that your husband was a flirt. You knew him better than I did. You know the truth."

"Yes, I know the truth, and it does not favor you." She swipes a hand across her eyes to get rid of her tears. "I'm glad you'll be getting what you deserve. Did you actually think you could get away with it?"

I shake my head. "I hit him only once. I never thought I killed him."

"You hit him hard enough to take his life, and you didn't tell a soul that you were with him that night. All that time you pretended to be concerned about me and my well-being, you were just trying to cover up your dirty secret." She snorts. "Every time you touched me, I felt disgusted. I know what you are. You are a dirty prostitute. You sleep with other people's husbands."

"I never." I swallow hard. "I was a stripper, not a prostitute."

How does she know about that part of my life? Did Jared tell her? Why would he if he had planned on keeping my past a secret for his own benefit? There are still so many pieces of the puzzle missing. Nothing makes sense to me anymore.

"No, you *are* a prostitute, and a murderer. You

killed my husband and you tried to kill yours. For that, you will rot in prison."

Through my anger, fears, and frustrations, I find a sliver of relief. She doesn't know everything. She doesn't know that I was in prison. If she did, she would have gone straight to the cops with the information. But it won't be long before my biggest secret is revealed. As soon as Jared recovers, he'll talk and my story will be all over the news.

"Fine, Rachel," I say. "You said what you came to say. I need you to leave." I blink my eyes several times before focusing on her face again. "But before you do, I need you to know that I'm truly sorry. I'm sorry that you had a husband like Victor. I know you want to hang on to the belief that he was a good husband, but I'm sorry to disappoint you. He knew that I used to be a stripper and he threatened to expose my secret unless I slept with him. When I refused, he forced himself on me. Whether you or anyone else believes it or not, it's the truth." I leave out the part about the baby because I don't want her to hurt more than she already is. Her anger comes from a place of pain, the kind of pain I would never wish on anyone.

I'm about to think of something else to say to her, when a sharp sensation spreads across my cheek. "Shut up," she says. "You are a liar. You seduced my husband. You killed him because you were afraid he would destroy your perfect little life."

The cops clearly saw her slap me, but instead of intervening, they continue to stare. I guess they think I deserve it.

Rachel is so furious that her face is puce and her body is shaking uncontrollably. "I hope you rot in hell. You stole my life from me and now you're going away for a long time." She wipes her eyes again. "Don't think you're safe in here. I was told you will probably be released tonight so you can be thrown behind bars. I hope they send you to a prison far away from this town. You don't belong here." With that, she storms out.

Outside the room, Officer Rogers gives her a quick hug and she disappears.

Not long after, he walks in, a silent smirk on his face. "Are you all right?" he asks.

I lay a palm on my aching cheek. "I'm pretty sure you're not in the least interested in my well-being, officer."

He doesn't have to pretend anymore. We both know whose side he's on. It's definitely not mine.

"As I mentioned before, Victor Hanes was my friend."

"So, what are you waiting for? If you believe I murdered him, why don't you take me to prison already?"

After two days in the hospital, my body is still in pain, but not the kind I won't be able to handle. Prison is the last place I'd rather be, but I'd feel safer behind bars than in the same hospital as Jared.

I saw him burn. I heard his cries of agony. But as long as I haven't seen the extent of his injuries with my own eyes, I won't feel safe.

Earlier, I asked the nurse about him again and she could not tell me much, except to repeat that he's still in critical condition. I wanted to see him, not because I care, but because I wanted to prove he no longer has the power to harm me. Even though I'm his wife, my request to visit his room was denied. On the other side of the coin, the officers and hospital staff probably think I'm a danger to him. I was the one who allegedly set him on fire.

Officer Rogers is about to speak when his phone rings. He holds up a finger and takes the call. His eyes remain on my face as he listens to the caller, then he frowns and glances at his partner through the partition.

"Okay," he says, "I'm on my way."

"What's going on?" I ask, looking from him to his partner. "Does it have something to do with me?"

"Someone broke into your house," he says and walks out of my room without an explanation.

I watch as he says something to his partner before running off in a hurry.

The other officer makes a call probably to ask for more information. When he's done, I call for him. He hesitates before entering the room.

"Please tell me what's going on. I deserve to know."

"All I know is that someone broke into your house about an hour ago. One of your neighbors reported seeing someone sneaking in. We should know more in a few hours." He walks out again. Unlike Officer Rogers, he's not interested in holding much of a conversation with me.

I'm confused as I stare through the window into the darkness, wondering whether the person who broke into the house was random or if it's someone Jared and I know. But the bigger question is, what did they want?

CHAPTER 37

The day after Rachel's visit, Nurse Julie informs me that the time has come for me to be discharged from the hospital.

My destination is prison and I should be panicking, but as I slide my feet into a pair of old slippers one of the nurses gave me, I'm strangely calm.

"Ready to leave, love?" Nurse Julie asks, walking into the room with one of her bright smiles. She makes it look as though this is a normal situation and instead of prison, I'm headed home. But she has been kind to me, unlike some of the others who gave me weird looks and whispered about me when they thought I was sleeping, debating about how long they think my prison sentence will be. By now, the entire town probably knows about me.

Since being at the hospital, I have refused to watch any TV or read the local paper, but I have a pretty good idea of what everyone thinks. I've heard loud noises outside my window, noises that reminded me of my past, people begging for justice to be served.

"Yes, I'm ready," I lie. I'll never be ready to hand over my freedom again. The one thing that comforts me is knowing I'll be away from Jared, behind bars where he can never hurt me again.

"That's lovely." Nurse Julie proceeds to tell me how to take care of myself so I recover fully. I listen to only half of what she says.

Finally, she helps me stand and I wince at the pain on the soles of my feet from being pierced by shards of glass and the thorns of Rachel's rosebushes. I grit my teeth to try and contain it.

From the other side of the glass, Officer Rogers is watching me with a blank expression. We haven't spoken to each other since he told me that Jared's house was broken into. He hasn't bothered to update me on what they found out and I didn't ask. It was probably a random break-in and I don't care what the thief took. It's not my home anymore and nothing in it belongs to me. It all belongs to a life I'm desperate to leave behind.

"Take care of yourself." The nurse reaches out to touch my hand.

I fool myself into believing she cares, and that she believes in my innocence. There must be people out there who do.

"Thank you." I give her a watery smile.

When she walks out, I expect Officer Rogers to burst into the room to slap the handcuffs on. But he's on the phone now, pacing and looking agitated as he speaks. After he hangs up, he stares at me for a long time.

My stomach twists.

Does he know? Has he found out that I was in prison before for murder?

Does it even matter anymore? I'm going to prison, possibly for life. One more crime added to my name won't make a difference.

Officer Rogers and his partner talk to each other for a long time. I wish I could hear what they're saying. Eventually, the partner nods and walks away while Officer Rogers makes his way to the door, his face a mask of what looks like shock.

"Let's go," he says in a voice that's much deeper than the one I'm used to.

I stretch out my hands for him to handcuff me.

"Not necessary," he says and gestures for me to follow him.

I clutch my discharge papers tight and hurry to his side. While people in the hallway stare at me, he puts a firm hand around my arm.

I bow my head so I don't meet anyone's eyes. The walk to the glass doors of the hospital takes forever in my mind, but in truth, it's only a few minutes.

When we reach the entrance, my fears return and my body forces me to come to a halt.

Officer Rogers nudges me a little, and I start walking again.

I'm glad he didn't handcuff me. The humiliation would have been too much to bear.

Outside the building is chaos. Chanting people are everywhere. They're holding signs and calling out my name. The word murderer is tossed around like a ping pong ball. I cover my ear with my hand to try and block out the noises, something a child would do.

As Officer Rogers pushes me through the crowd, one of his hands rested in the space between my shoulder blades, something lands on my cheek and starts sliding down my skin. It's not the first time someone has spat on me. It hurts as much as it did back then.

"Keep moving," Officer Rogers says over the noise while urging people to make way.

We finally make it to the police car, and he guides me into the backseat and slams the door shut.

Hands slap my window and fists hit the top of the car, making me jump.

I sigh with relief when Officer Rogers gets behind the wheel. I want to get away from the angry crowd, but I'm sure more people will be waiting at our destination. That's how it was last time.

After a few honks of the car horn, the vehicle lurches forward and protesters jump out of the way.

"Are you all right back there?" Officer Rogers asks when we finally leave the angry crowd behind.

"Yeah," I say. Why does he care? If he weren't a cop, he'd probably be among the people begging for my severe punishment. The people of Sanlow stick together.

They were right all along. They speculated that it was an outsider who had killed Victor Hanes. I *am* an outsider to them.

I close my eyes to block out images of me inside a stinking jail cell, huddled in a corner like an animal, but the memories flood back all at once, memories of the first day I was thrown behind bars.

I remember being fingerprinted and photographed, and the weight of my new folded uniform as it was placed in my arms.

When I open my eyes, I notice that we're not headed in the direction of the police station. Even as an outsider, I'm familiar with the town.

"Are you taking me to a jail out of town?" I ask. Sanlow is a small town, where crimes of this magnitude hardly happen, and the authorities might not have sufficient resources to handle my case.

"You're going where you belong," he says,

staring straight ahead. "Would you like something to drink? I have an extra Coke, but it's pretty warm."

I shake my head. "I'm not thirsty...thanks."

"How are you feeling?" His tone is surprisingly gentle.

"Fine." I narrow my eyes in suspicion. "Why are you being nice to me?"

"I'm a nice person by nature," he says, throwing a quick glance at me.

"But you weren't nice to me before."

"Yeah. That's because as a cop, I'm not a huge fan of criminals."

"But I'm still a criminal in your eyes." I should stop talking. Conversing with a cop without a lawyer present could end up working against me. But I can't stop myself.

He doesn't respond, so I change the subject. "Did you find out who broke into the house?"

"*Your* house, you mean?"

"No, the house I used to live in. It was never my house. It's Jared Bloom's house."

He glances at me again with a perplexed expression. "No, we don't know who broke in yet. We're still looking into it."

"Do you think they took anything?"

"I wouldn't know. I don't know what was there before. You might have to have a look around your house and let us know if anything is missing."

A bitter laugh escapes my lips. "We both know that I'll never enter that house again."

He says nothing. Instead of continuing our conversation, he turns on the radio to a classical music station, a message to me that the conversation is over.

I'm glad when he opens the windows to let fresh air in, replacing the stench of cigarettes and sweat.

I close my eyes again, trying to calm my nerves. It's a good thing we'll be on the road for a while. It will give me time to prepare my mind for what's to come. As darkness falls behind my eyelids, I try not to think of anything. Not the barbed wire on the prison fence, not a damp prison cell that smells of mildew, not the sound of metal hitting metal. I focus on the sound of my heart beating and fall asleep without planning to.

I wake up to the sounds of screaming and a lot of shouting.

As soon as my eyes adjust, I realize that we are on Montlake Street, and all around us are people.

"What...why are we here?"

"Because this is your home," Officer Rogers says, opening the door and helping me out of the car, his hand around my upper arm as he had done at the hospital.

Two other police cars are parked on our street. There are not as many protesters present and I don't see any signs with my name on them. But what I *do* see throws me for a loop.

"I don't understand. What's going on?" I ask, my senses spinning out of control.

Rachel is standing between two police officers, screaming at them. When she turns her head, our eyes meet from across the distance. She gets even more hysterical, trying to free herself from the cops. I watch in shock as handcuffs are slapped onto her wrists.

Officer Rogers doesn't answer my question until he has brought me to the doorstep. He turns to me with a smile that looks genuine. "Kelsey Bloom, you're free to go. We found evidence that you did not kill Victor Hanes. Someone else finished the job."

"Rachel?" My eyes are still on her as a police officer puts a hand on top of her head to lower her into the vehicle. "She did it? How?" My mind is reeling with confusion.

"That's what we're about to find out." He pauses. "Take care of yourself, Mrs. Bloom."

"I'm really free? But what about Jared? I was being accused of setting him on fire." Why the hell am I trying to remind him of my crimes? I guess it's my mind trying to make sense of everything that's happening too fast. I was so convinced I was going to prison.

"We know it was self-defense. Some of your neighbors confirmed that they heard you

308

screaming several times that night. Someone also saw your husband attacking you through your dining room window. There was also a receipt to prove he bought the gasoline. You were only trying to save your own life."

"I can't believe it," I say, sinking onto the doorstep, too weak to stand.

"You better believe it." He glances at his watch. "I have to go. But we might contact you if we need any more information. For now, make sure you get the doors and windows repaired, and take care of the fire damage. If you see anything suspicious, call us immediately."

I don't say anything as I stare at the police car with a hysterical Rachel in the backseat. She's out of control, slamming the back of her head against the headrest. Even though the windows are closed, I can hear her screams.

Once the police cars drive off, people start to disperse and I'm left reeling from the sudden rush of both relief and confusion.

I feel like someone who had been drowning only to be pulled out of the water without warning. I'm gasping for air as I learn to breathe again.

CHAPTER 38

I'm standing at the kitchen door, observing the scene after the fire. It's pretty bad. Every surface is covered in black. The smell of smoke still lingers in the air.

I'm finding it hard to believe that I survived it all, that Jared didn't get away with murder yet again.

"Hello," someone calls from behind me. I jump and whirl around.

"Linda," I breathe. "You scared me. I didn't hear—"

"Sorry. I didn't mean to startle you. Your door is...broken." She takes a step closer to me. "Poor Kelsey, how are you?" She places a hand on my shoulder, but I can see her peering past me into the kitchen.

Her fake sympathy doesn't fool me. She's only looking for information in order to feed the Sanlow gossip mill.

"I'm fine." When I say nothing more, her

smile wavers.

"Look, you've been through so much. Is there anything I can do? You could come over for a coffee."

"No, I'm not staying long. I'm leaving town. I'm just here to pack a bag." I'll never be able to sleep in the house I was tortured in. Every corner reminds me of Jared and how close I came to death's door.

Linda nods her head. "I totally understand that you would not want to see anyone right now. But you must sit down for a moment. You look like you're about to faint." She puts an arm around my shoulders and leads me to the living room.

I'm much too exhausted to resist.

As soon as I'm settled on the couch, she sits down next to me. "I can't believe Rachel killed her own husband and tried to pin it on you."

"How do you know she did it?"

"She pretty much admitted it in front of everyone." Linda places a hand on her chest. "When the cops showed up and confronted her, she started shouting that her husband was a cheater and that he didn't deserve to live. I've never seen that kind of anger before."

Even though I would rather be alone, maybe having Linda over is not such a bad idea. She can fill in some of the blanks in my mind.

"How did the cops find out that it was her in

the first place? Did they just show up out of nowhere?"

"From what I hear, they received an anonymous call. They all showed up an hour ago and started searching the house. I went over there thinking Rachel might need me, but she was running around like a mad woman. She kicked me out. I've never seen her like that. She was a completely different person."

"An anonymous caller? Why would they wait until now to make the call?"

"I don't know," Linda says.

"Do you know how she apparently killed Victor?"

"No. The cops refused to talk. I only overheard conversations here and there. I was ordered to stand back while they did their job. But I'm guessing she had some help. She's a small woman and Victor was a big man. How did she get his body into the water?"

As soon as Linda stops talking, the wheels inside my mind start turning. I dip my head to the side. "Linda, the night that Victor disappeared, how did she seem when you went to see her?"

"Who? Rachel?"

"Yes. Jared mentioned that you and Don went to check up on her."

"That's weird," Linda says, frowning. "We never went to Rachel's house that night. But you're right, Jared did. I was at the kitchen window when I saw him ring the doorbell. It wasn't long after they both left the house and walked down the street. I found it strange, but when we later found out about Victor's disappearance, it was clear that he was trying to comfort her." Linda chews on a cuticle. "Rachel was such a great actress. She fooled us all. I don't even feel like I know her."

"Yeah," I say absentmindedly. Everything is becoming clearer. I have no doubt now that Jared was involved in some way. How else would he have a video that both of them saw?

Maybe Rachel killed Victor and asked Jared to help her get rid of the body. She must have filmed the video and showed it to Jared. If she told someone that another man slept with me, Victor and Jared's deal would be off.

What I don't know is whether Jared offered Rachel money to keep her quiet. Or maybe he threatened to tell the cops what she did if she didn't keep her mouth shut.

"If you don't mind me asking, what happened between you and Jared?" Linda takes my hand. "I always thought of you two as the perfect couple. But I heard he kept you prisoner."

"He did," I say truthfully. There's no point in hiding the truth from anyone anymore. They need to see Jared for the person he is. "It was awful. He locked me up in the basement. That night, he tried to set me on fire, but ended up getting burned instead." I burst into tears and Linda puts her arms around me. I no longer care if she's going to tell everyone my story, that she heard it firsthand.

"I'm sorry, Kelsey." Linda tightens her arms around my body. "If it hurts too much, you don't have to say anything more."

I'm so shocked about her words that I pull back. There are tears in her eyes.

"My grandfather abused my grandmother up until his death," she says. "He did terrible things to her, including kicking her in the ribs until they were broken. She never left him. You were brave enough to fight back."

"Thank you, Linda, for sharing that with me."

"Are you really leaving town?" Linda dabs the tears from her cheeks with her fingertips.

"Yes, but only after the cops tell me it's fine for me to leave. They might have more questions about Jared. If you don't mind me asking, how is Don doing?" I inspect my fingernails. "I mean, Jared is his friend. How is he handling it?"

"Surprisingly well. For some reason, he seems to be in a rather good mood."

Of course, he is. Since Jared and Victor are no longer getting the money, it all goes to him.

"Do you think he will defend Jared in court?" I ask.

"I don't think so. We have actually talked

about leaving town as well, but not right away. This town is no longer the same for us. It's tainted."

I nod. They want to start a new life in another place with all their money. I can't help wondering whether Linda knows about it. But I don't care. All I care about is that I have my freedom back, and if all goes well, the cops will not find out that I'm on the run.

After Linda leaves, I search the house for my phone. I find it in Jared's office, tucked at the back of a drawer. While it's charging, I throw a few necessities into a bag.

It suddenly dawns on me that I have no money. I can't even afford to sleep in a motel.

I sink down onto the bed and glare at the handcuffs that still hang from the headboard, a nasty memory.

After staring at the handcuffs for a while, I search the room for my backpack to see if my purse is still inside. I don't find it. Jared must have hidden it somewhere or thrown it away. He probably also locked me out of the account I had access to.

When my phone has charged enough, I switch it on and go online. My stomach is in knots as I type in my old name.

Lacie Pullman

I haven't searched for that name in months. I worked so hard to forget, to pretend the person I used to be never existed, to live my life as if I didn't have a dark past.

What I read about her in the online articles is not what I expected.

My heart is pounding as I click on the first one from a year ago.

Shocking new update on the Granny murderer...

Lacie Pullman, who was believed to have murdered her grandmother at the age of seventeen, has still not been found. According to the authorities, she escaped while being transferred to a Missoula hospital for treatment. The police vehicle was involved in an accident that killed both of the guards escorting her, but Lacie was never seen again.

Some believe she died that night, that maybe she managed to escape from the vehicle, but later succumbed to her injuries. The question is, where is her corpse?

If Lacie died that night, she will never know about the shocking twist in her case.

Two weeks ago, Amy Pierce, an elderly woman dying of cancer, who claims to have been friends with Lacie's grandmother, Adeline Pullman, came forward to prove that Lacie was sent to prison for a crime she did not commit, a crime she spent ten years in prison for.

According to the local authorities, she had sufficient evidence to prove that Lacie's grandmother had carefully planned her own death and had wanted from the start to blame it on her granddaughter.

As the words sink in, my phone slips from my hand and drops to the floor. I pick it up again and read the article all over again. It's not real. It can't be real. Too much good can't happen to me all at once.

I return to the search engine in search for more articles. They all report the same story. Even one of the cops who had led the investigation admitted I was innocent.

If only I had known all this before, I would never have gone through everything that I did. I would never have worked as a stripper. I would never have met Garry or Jared. I would have lived a completely different life.

Maybe I would not even have known the pain of losing a child.

In a daze, I stumble out of the bedroom and return to Jared's office. I drop into his leather desk chair. My stomach turns immediately. Everything smells of him. The scent is powerful enough to awaken all the unpleasant memories.

To shut them out, I close my eyes and lean forward to rest my forehead on the desk, the place he would normally put his laptop. My head snaps up.

His laptop. It's not on the desk. Maybe the cops took it. Like a growing seed, the need to see the video Jared had shown me unfurls to life inside of me.

It's over. I'm free. But Jared is not yet behind bars. I'm not even sure whether, after he recovers, he will be sent to prison. He's a dangerous man. If they let him go, I won't be safe. Any woman who comes into contact with him will be in danger.

I need more evidence to make sure he doesn't hurt me again. I need to secure my newfound freedom.

I rise from the chair and turn in circles, studying the room that's no longer as immaculate as it used to be, on days when Jared wasn't throwing a fit. The cops must have already searched it, shifting things around. Or was it the person who broke in?

What did the person want? When I entered the house, I didn't notice anything missing.

What if it was Rachel? What if Jared had some kind of evidence that worked against her?

My gut tells me it was her. Maybe she was looking for the video. Did she find it? If not, it might still be inside the house, inside the office.

There's not much in the room aside from a desk that stands on a black and white rug, a mahogany chest of drawers against the wall next to the window, and an exercise bike.

I start with the desk, yanking open drawers and spilling the contents onto the floor.

Among the bills and other paperwork pertaining to the house, I find nothing that can help me.

I search every surface, every corner. I find nothing that could help nail Jared for good, but inside a small drawer, I come across several dollar bills, coins, crumpled tissues, a restaurant receipt, and a key ring. He must have emptied his pockets into it.

The money will help pay for at least two nights at a motel while I decide what to do and where to go.

The sound of the landline ringing makes me freeze. I shuffle to the living room, my mind trying to guess who the caller is.

The ringing stops before I can answer. I don't expect the phone to ring again. When it does, I let out a silent gasp of surprise.

I blow out a breath and grab it again before it stops.

"Hello? This is...Kelsey Bloom speaking."

"You have a collect call from Rosemary White. Would you like to accept?"

CHAPTER 39

I've been sitting across from Rosemary for five minutes, unsure what to say to her. The prison clock is ticking. Our time together will be over soon. But what can I say to the woman who betrayed me? Hearing she was locked up also knocked the wind from my lungs.

She didn't want to tell me why she was behind bars on the phone. She begged to see me in person. As soon as we came face to face, her eyes landed on my stomach, but she said nothing. Does she know the baby is gone? I'm glad she doesn't ask. I wouldn't want to put the pain of losing a baby into words.

I don't recognize her. Her hair is tangled around her head and the area around her eyes is so swollen, making it hard to look into them.

She finally speaks.

"I'm sorry," she says in a broken whisper. "I didn't mean to hurt you."

"Why? Why did you do it? And why are you

in prison?"

"I did some terrible things in my life."

"Start at the beginning," I say. "I'm tired of being lied to."

"Jared is my son," she blurts out.

I stare at her, baffled. "What do you mean he's your son?"

"He's...I raised him. He's my son."

"You adopted him?" My voice sounds calm, but inside me, my emotions are at war.

Rosemary closes her eyes and takes a breath. "No, I stole him."

My head snaps back. "You what?"

She meets my gaze again. "I only wanted to help." A tear trickles down her lined face. "His biological mother was my neighbor. She was not fit to be a mother, and I couldn't have kids of my own. I was desperate for a child. Adoption was too expensive and complicated."

"You took him without his mother's permission?" I bury my hands in my hair. "You stole him? I can't believe this."

"I wanted to protect him. That's all I wanted." She presses her lips together. "I didn't know that he...he's a bad person."

"Oh, my God." I had no idea I was caught up in a web more complicated than I could have ever imagined. "Why didn't you tell me this?"

"He didn't want anyone to know." Rosemary bows her head. "He was a tough kid to raise.

When he found out what I did, he became even more damaged. He stole from me, lied, and manipulated me every chance he got." She glances at the guard in the room. "I stuck by him because he was my problem. I brought him into my life. It was my punishment for what I did."

"Have you always lived here? Does anyone in town know?"

Rosemary shakes her head. "This is my hometown, but I left when I was eighteen to study in New York. After college, I met someone and stayed."

"You were married?" I'm suddenly curious to know everything about her. Jared *did* mention to me that his mother was from Sanlow. I could never have guessed it was Rosemary. He told me his parents were dead.

"Yes." Rosemary folds her hands on the scarred table. "But when my husband found out what I did, he left me. Jared and I left New York because the police were searching for him."

"Your ex-husband never reported you?"

"When he asked me for a divorce, he said he wouldn't. But he did say God will punish me for what I did. I guess he was right. Having Jared in my life was like a curse. He caused trouble everywhere. He threw tantrums almost every day and was kicked out of school more times than I can count. We moved a lot."

"Did he ever lay a hand on you?" When

Rosemary speaks about Jared, her gaze darts around the room as if she's afraid he might show up.

She gives a small nod. "He was violent. He harmed other kids and animals." She glances down at her right hand, studying the angry scar carved into her skin. I know now that Jared is responsible for it. "A doctor I took him to said his behavior could be linked to an imbalance in critical brain chemicals. When he left to attend college in New York, I was relieved. I didn't feel safe with him in the house. I wanted him gone. When he finally left, I opened up the shelter."

She waits for me to speak, but I'm still reeling from her confession.

"The Rosemary Home was my way of making up for what I did. I should never have taken Jared." Rosemary is wringing her hands now. I can only imagine how hard it is for her to tell me her story. "When he showed up in town as a man with a different name, I wanted to believe he had changed, but then the threats started again. He threatened to tell the cops that I stole even more babies and sold them to mothers who couldn't get pregnant. He had always been a good liar. The cops would have believed him."

My head is ringing from everything I'm hearing. It sickens me to know that Jared was even more evil than I thought.

"I'm sorry you went through all that." As a

normal person, I'm tempted to hold on to my anger, to punish Rosemary for what she did to me, but we both suffered at the hands of Jared.

"No, I'm sorry. I shouldn't have allowed him to manipulate me into luring you to town."

"Did you know why he asked you to do it? Did he explain?"

"He said it was none of my business. I was so stupid." She reaches out to touch my hand, but the guard coughs. She withdraws it again. "I wanted to help you get away from him, but when he found out that you came to me for help, he came to my house and tried to strangle me. He warned that if I meddled in his business again, the next time he would finish the job."

I wrap a hand around my throat, imagining Jared's hands around my neck. "Did you know about his former wife?"

"I never knew he was married. During the years he was away, we didn't have any contact at all. He never even called me for money. But he was a good thief and master manipulator. He must have stolen whatever he needed." Rosemary sighs. "When I told the cops that I raised him, they questioned me about her...the ex-wife. The officer said he's being accused of murdering her."

I nod.

"And he hurt you. It's all my fault." Rosemary can no longer hold back her tears.

"No," I say firmly, wishing I could pull her into my arms and comfort her the way she used to comfort me. "It's not your fault. It's not my fault. It's all on Jared."

"You forgive me?" she asks.

"I...maybe one day." I peel my gaze from hers. The wounds are still too fresh.

"I wanted to make it up to you. That's why I called the cops."

"You were the anonymous caller?" I straighten up.

"One of the times Jared came to see me, the day he tried to strangle me, he got a call from someone named Rachel. He said her name several times."

"Did you hear anything else?"

"Yes. He was assuring her that no one will find out, and that she should stop going to the lake. He told her to trust him."

"Rachel was Victor's wife," I say.

"I know that now. When I saw her name in the papers, I remembered the phone call and put two and two together."

"She was arrested for the murder."

"But that doesn't mean Jared is innocent. He was involved in some way." She pauses. "Why else would he have the video?"

"The video?" I lean forward. "What video?"

She averts her gaze. "I was the one who broke into your house. I wanted to find something...anything that would help get Jared arrested. I found his phone inside one of his jacket pockets. When I saw the video, I knew he was involved."

"Is that why you're in here?" Surely, it can't be for kidnapping Jared. There must be some statute of limitations.

She nods. "I turned myself in and handed the phone to the cops. I'm also locked up because Jared *did* tell the cops that I'm a child kidnapper. He kept his promise. Apparently, he called them the night he tried to set you on fire."

When I was trapped inside the bathroom, I heard Jared talking. Was he talking to the cops, telling them about Rosemary? I guess he was determined to destroy both of the women in his life.

"I didn't kidnap any more babies. You have to believe me, Kelsey."

"I believe you," I say as the guard signals that our time is up.

"I left money for you," Rosemary says as she's taken away. "Contact my lawyer, Aaron Sailor. I hope you'll forgive me one day."

I try to say something, but my throat is clogged by tears. Rosemary is taken away, and I'm left to figure out what comes next.

CHAPTER 40

I'm standing in the Sanlow Cemetery and Rosemary's casket is being lowered into the ground. Two days after I visited her, I received a call from her lawyer that she had suffered a heart attack. I spent the rest of the day sitting in bed, weeping for the woman she was before I found out that she had betrayed me. I also wept for the woman who had been hurt and betrayed by Jared.

The day the call came in, I had planned to leave town. I had already packed everything, and opened a bank account for the lawyer to transfer the eight thousand dollars Rosemary had gifted me, her way of apologizing.

When it's my turn to throw a white rose onto the casket, sobs overwhelm me again. All Rosemary wanted was my forgiveness, and I did not give it to her. When I visited her, I was too bruised that it felt right to hold on to the grudge for longer. Now I regret it. I should have said the words.

As soon as she told me about the things Jared did to her, most of the anger I had been harboring toward her melted away. I knew I would forgive her, maybe I already had. Now it's too late. She will never hear the words she wanted me to say.

My rose hits the casket with a soft thud. I step away, walking into the arms of Phylis, one of the Rosemary Home staff members.

"She loved you," Phylis says, smoothing my hair. "Never forget that."

I pull back and give her a sad smile. "I loved her too." Even though we were manipulated into crossing each other's paths, she was the mother I never had.

"Will you come with us to the shelter?" Phylis asks as we walk to our cars. "We're having a small lunch only for the staff."

I shake my head. "I'm sorry, I can't. I'm actually leaving town right now."

"That's a shame." She stops and hugs me again. "I wish you all the best, Kelsey. You deserve to be happy now. Stop by for a visit if you're ever in town."

"I will," I say even though I don't see myself returning to Sanlow.

I wave goodbye to everyone and get behind the wheel of my car.

I told Phylis that I'll be leaving town

immediately, but I don't. Instead, I make a quick stop at the hospital.

I never want to see Jared again, but I need some kind of closure so I can move forward with my life.

My knees are weak as I'm escorted to his room, where two cops I have never met before are standing. I introduce myself to them and they let me enter.

The man I once knew is no longer there, only a bundle wrapped in bandages. Most of his body is covered in white including his face. But his eyes and mouth are visible and that's enough for me.

He doesn't open his eyes until I approach his bed and look down at him.

The green in his eyes has dimmed. They look almost lifeless.

As our eyes meet, his tongue slides from his mouth to wet his lips, which move apart slightly as if he wants to say something. Nothing comes out.

"Your mother was buried today," I say. "Rosemary may not have been your biological mother, but she raised you. She put up with your nonsense, and what did you do? You hurt her. You're responsible for her death." My gaze sweeps across his body. "I wish you a quick recovery, Jared. The sooner you heal, the sooner you can go to prison where you belong. You will never hurt anyone again."

I spoke to Officer Rogers the day I visited Rosemary. He said enough evidence was found on Jared's laptop to charge him for the murder of his ex-wife in addition to the attempted murder.

His lips part again. This time he croaks out three words. "Go to hell."

"No, that's not part of my plans. I'm leaving town to start a new life as a free woman. You, on the other hand, will soon be given a one-way ticket to hell. Goodbye, Jared."

When I walk out of the building, it feels like a heavy weight has been lifted off my shoulders. But there's still something else I need to do.

Inside my car, I pull a letter from my new purse and smooth it out on my lap. Linda gave it to me when I had coffee with her this morning.

Dear Kelsey,

I called you several times. I was hoping you would visit me so we can speak in person, but I understand why you refuse to see me again.

I don't expect you to forgive me after the things I did to you.

The only good thing about being inside a jail cell is that I have enough time to think. I've spent many hours thinking about you.

My ego hates to admit this, but you were right and I was wrong. My husband hurt you and I blamed you for it. It was wrong. I see that now. I was so angry with Victor that I took it out on you. For that, I'm terribly sorry.

The day he raped you, we had a huge fight and he walked out. He said he needed some air. After a while, I followed him in the hopes that we could make up. I was ovulating. I needed us to make peace so we could try again to make a baby. Then I saw the things he was doing to you. I recorded it all because I actually wanted to report him to the cops, but then my anger got out of control. After you hit him and ran away, I went to him.

I don't remember how it happened. I just remember holding a bloody stone in my hand. I panicked and felt for a pulse, but he was gone. I killed my own husband, not you. I didn't know what to do, so I called Jared. He promised to help me if I never told anyone what happened that day.

But it was hard to forget. Every time I saw you, I saw my husband raping you. I made myself believe it was your fault. You were a stripper—not a prostitute—at one point in your life. I found that out while going through some of Victor's stuff. He had a whole folder on you. He must have had some sick obsession with you.

I sent you all those notes and the text messages because I wanted you gone, especially after I found out about the pregnancy. I saw you buy the pregnancy test. I knew it was Victor's. Victor told me once that Jared can't have kids. You cannot even imagine how much it hurt to see your stomach growing with my husband's baby.

I thought if you left town, it would be easier for me to forget what happened. But Jared brought you back. At the time, I didn't understand why he would want you. In my eyes, you were tainted. I now know that he was obsessed with you in his own twisted way.

I'm sorry I didn't help you when I heard your screams. As a woman, I'm ashamed of myself.

You don't have to forgive me, but please understand that I was not myself. I was drowning in too much pain.

I'm going to prison for murder, but I think I deserve to be punished for so much more, for the things I did to you.

Linda told me you're leaving town. I hope you find a better life wherever you're going.

Goodbye, Kelsey.

Rachel

P.S. For all it's worth, I never told the cops about you

being in prison before. I hope they never find out.

When I finish reading, I fold the letter up again and push it into my purse.

I'm a free woman now. I'm free from Jared, Victor, and even Garry. According to Rosemary's lawyer, who I told about my past, Garry is back behind bars where he belongs. After looking into my case, the lawyer also confirmed my innocence. I did not kill my grandmother.

With tears of gratitude in my eyes, I drive out of Sanlow to search for my own version of a perfect life.

THE END

Thank you for reading *The Midnight Wife*. If you enjoyed this book, please leave a review.

To be notified when L.G. Davis releases a new book, visit www.author-lgdavis.com to sign up for her newsletter.

OTHER BOOKS BY L.G. DAVIS

Don't Blink

To get in touch with L.G. Davis visit:
www.author-lgdavis.com
Email: Liz@lizgdavis.com

Made in the USA
Coppell, TX
30 November 2022

87450208R00194